STUCK IN THE MIDDLE

"Here you are, Mister Gunn," said Leni, bringing a dusty bottle of brandy and a cigar.

"It's just Gunn," he said, for perhaps the tenth time.

"Bring us two glasses," Kristina added, "and a match for Mister Gunn—I mean Gunn."

Both women laughed, and it sounded good. Leni brought the glasses.

"Well," Kristina continued, "Pa said you had a big reputation, but were not a bad man. He thought you might be the kind of man who would want to stick around, help us. I fought against it, but now I'm not sure that he wasn't right."

Gunn drew on his cigar, sipped more brandy. He had given it some thought. He couldn't just leave them here, their pa being dead and all. They didn't know how to hunt, and the Rockies were merciless. It was a young man's job, not a woman's. He knew the mountains. But knowing the mountains took time. And these two sisters didn't have time.

"Damn," Gunn muttered. "What in the hell have I got myself into this time?"

Kristina and Leni sat staring at him with hopelessly big brown eyes.

Gunn was stuck.

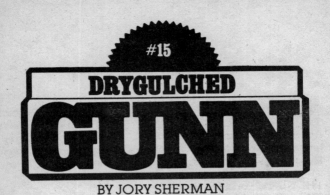

#15

DRYGULCHED
GUNN

BY JORY SHERMAN

ZEBRA BOOKS
KENSINGTON PUBLISHING CORP.

For Bob Millsap,
writer & friend

ZEBRA BOOKS

are published by

KENSINGTON PUBLISHING CORP.
475 Park Avenue South
New York, N.Y. 10016

Copyright © 1983 by Jory Sherman

Printed in the United States of America

CHAPTER ONE

The big sorrel stepped with an easy gait along the trail, its rider dozing in the saddle. Suddenly its ears pricked, stood up stiff, alert. It halted, jolting Gunn away. Its rubbery nostrils sniffed as its ears twisted to pick up any alien sound.

Gunn scanned his unfamiliar surroundings, his senses prickling with a spidery sensitivity.

Something was out of kilter. Esquire was stiff as a rail fence under him, his neck bowed for battle.

"What is it boy? You see something?"

Esquire, sixteen and a half hands high, blew a riffle of air through his nose, stamped the ground with his forefoot.

Seconds later, Gunn heard the metallic click of a breech opening. Then, before he could react, the clunk, clunk of the breech closing, the lever locking in its groove. Instinctively, he ducked, bending over the saddle, hugging Esquire's neck and mane.

A rifle cracked. A bullet sizzled over his head, sending shivers up his spine. Esquire half-reared, backing away from the sound, the smell of black powder. Gunn reached for the Winchester in its scabbard, drew it swiftly even as he heard the click, clunk, clunk of the lever-action arming for another shot.

"Easy, boy," he muttered to the horse, reining him into position. He handled the Winchester with one hand, brought it up so he could cock it. He wrapped the reins around the saddle horn with his left hand, reached for the cocking lever. The seconds crawled. He felt weighted down as his mind screamed: too slow, too damned slow!

A second shot boomed so close his ears rang.

The bullet smacked into the barrel of the Winchester. His hand stung with the vibration, the impact of the lead ball hitting it with muscle-wrenching foot-pounds of energy. Pain shot through his wrist.

Esquire backed away, working the bit in his mouth, biting it in fear.

Gunn forced himself into cocking the Winchester. He swung the rifle as a third shot blasted the silence, so fast on the heels of the second he could scarcely believe only one man was shooting at him. The bullet slammed into the receiver of the Winchester with deadly accuracy. Pain jolted through his wrists and arms. The rifle was wrenched from his grasp, fell to the ground, clattering on stones.

In the trees, he saw a single shadow, darting to another position.

Gunn clawed for his .45 Colt as Esquire backed into the pines bordering the opposite side of the trail. The bushwacker fired again. Bark flew from a tree inches from Gunn's face, spattering his face, nicking one eye at the corner. He blinked, as the sudden tears washed the alien substance onto his cheek. He cocked the .45, sent a shot rattling through the trees on the opposite side of the road. He fired just under the last puff of white smoke knowing that the chances of hitting an unseen target were about as good as a pair of deuces in a high-draw poker game.

Gunn drew in a breath, sought better cover. He inched Esquire deeper into the trees, held him behind a large pine. He waited, his blue-grey eyes, pale as pewter, flicking from left to right, trying to pick up movement. It grew quiet as he waited there, listening for any sound that might tell him where the rifleman had gone or was going. In the distance, a quail piped a warning. Another quail picked it up, passed it along, like a sentry on patrol. Then it was quiet again. Dead quiet.

The tall man with the pale eyes strained to hear, keeping Esquire perfectly still with pressure from his knees. His pistol was ready, cocked, the barrel tilted slightly upward, ready to drop on any visible target.

The next shot came from a totally different direction. He had not seen anyone cross the road, yet the bullet came from his flank. Esquire spooked as the bullet struck the tree in front of his nose. The splinters of pine bark stung his nose. He backed and reared. Gunn felt the animal twist out from under him. The next minute he was out of the saddle, diving for the dirt. His pistol went off aimlessly as his elbow struck the ground hard. Esquire danced away, snorting and stamping. A splinter stuck out of his nose; blood oozed from the cut.

Gunn lay there stunned, out of breath. He crawled behind the tree, tried to see through the smoke that hung in the air like a ghostly shroud. Even as he looked, he knew the ambusher had changed position again. He looked out toward the road, his rifle. That was the only chance he had. He needed the range, the steadiness of it, the good sights. He felt helpless, alone. Esquire had stopped moving, but his sounds had covered those of the bushwhacker.

Gunn crawled toward the road. A stand of aspen blocked his way, but he could use them for cover. He did not cock the pistol. Not yet. If the rifleman was circling him, he might make it to the road, dash across to the other side, picking up the Winchester on the way. It was worth a try. So far, the gunman had proved to be accurate if he meant to warn, not to kill. Of course he could be just a shade off, too. There was no way of knowing for sure.

Gunn reached the far edge of the aspen stand, stood upright. He started toward the rifle, looking up and down the trail. He took one step, heard the rifle boom again. The rifle skittered away, spun once as the lead ball spanged into the muzzle end of the barrel.

"Shit!" breathed Gunn.

He stooped, picked up a stone. He tossed it toward the road.

The hidden rifle spoke again. The stone blew apart in mid-air, disintegrated like a clay pigeon.

Here was no question in Gunn's mind now. The ambusher was a shooter. His scalp prickled, knowing that he was at the rifleman's mercy. He could have been killed long before now.

Why in hell was he being pinned down like this?

What did the man want? Was he playing with him like a cat with a mouse? It was a deadly business

8

nonetheless. It was no game. Not for him.

Gunn ran to a larger tree. The rifle sounded from still another position. The white bark of the aspen tree screeched as a chunk of it flew off, sailing like a pieplate in the air.

That time, however, Gunn had seen the fireflash. Now he knew where the man was.

Gunn waited for several seconds. It was time to see if the man meant to kill him or just scare him off. That last shot had been head high. The fresh scar on the aspen glared at him like an open wound.

Gunn slid his hat forward. Sweat-slick black hair gleamed in the sun as he let the hat fall over the barrel of his Colt single-action pistol. He edged the hat from behind the tree.

Metal clicked. A hammer cocked. The rifle barked. The hat spun on the barrel of Gunn's pistol. A hole appeared magically in the crown. Gunn pulled the pistol out from under it, stepped out from behind the tree. The drygulcher was in plain view, cocking the rifle for still another shot.

Gunn's eyes didn't even flicker as he thumbed back the hammer, fired, belt-high. The Colt bucked in his hand with a reassuring thrust of its rosewood grip. Smoke and orange flame belched from the six-inch barrel. He rode with the bullet all the way to its destination. The drygulcher shot backward a good foot and a half as the bullet slammed into his belly just above his beltbuckle.

His rifle dropped to the ground, stood on its butt for a minute before falling over with inertia. The man pitched forward, clutching his bleeding gut.

Gunn dashed toward him, cocking his Colt on the

run. He stood over the man, shoved a boot under him, flipped him onto his back. He put the pistol close to the man's eyes so there would be no mistaking his intent.

"Who in hell are you?" Gunn asked, his sensuous lips wet with saliva.

"Grandy Lund," the man groaned. A crimson stain spread slowly across his blue shirt.

"You shot at me. Why?"

The man's eyes glazed, went in and out of focus. Gunn knew he was dying.

"Thought you was one of those miners who've been poaching my meat. Well, ain't you?"

"I'm just passing through. What in hell do you mean 'your meat'? You ranching up here?"

"Hunter. Jesus, man, I'm dying. You gonna just stand there, watch me leak all over the ground?"

"Likely, you'll die. You got a place you want to go? If it's close you might make it. If you stay here you'll have a little more time to breathe."

"Up on the ridge." Lund moved his head, winced with pain. A blue coil of intestine started to ooze through the hole in his belly. He shoved it back in, gritting his teeth. "Got a cabin up there. Two daughters. I'm a meat hunter. Was. Looks like I got a couple of orphans to leave behind."

"They can't stay up there alone."

"Nope. One's almost eighteen, the other's bare twenty. I'm all they got."

Gunn cursed.

Lund's lips were starting to turn blue. His breathing was coarse, thready. He didn't have much time. The man was bearded, hazel-eyed, with a three-day beard stippling his face. Gunn took him to be about forty. His hair was long, tied back with a bandanna. His pants were buckskin. He wore boot moccasins that were unbeaded, worn, thick-padded at the soles. He carried a big knife and a pair of pistols that had seen use. He was big, rugged, or else he would have died quick. He didn't show the pain he must have been feeling and Gunn gave him credit for that. He wasn't a whiner. He thought only of his kids, who were about to be orphaned because of a damned foolish mistake.

"I'll whistle up my horse, try to pack you home. Hang on if you can, Lund."

Lund wheezed, closed his eyes.

"Hurry," he breathed. "Damn it's getting dark out here."

Gunn looked up, squinted into the blazing sun.

No, there wasn't much time for Grandy Lund.

CHAPTER TWO

Gunn could smell the man's death on his breath.

Yet he had seen men live with worse wounds. Grandy Lund was hardy, but the .45 ball had torn through a lot of flesh and gut. There was no telling how much damage had been done. The only good sign was that the ball hadn't torn out half his back. There was a small blue-edged hole in his belly, and a quarter-sized leak in his back. The bullet had missed the spine, probably deflected off a rib. A bullet after it was fired had its own damned mind.

Lund watched the tall man with the grey eyes as he found easier breathing the way Gunn had laid him out. He looked at the horse and wondered if he could ever get near it, much less get up on its back. The horse looked tall as a tree from his position.

"Going to pack those wounds before I move you," Gunn said.

"You already bandaged me."

"Keep you from leaking 'till I pack the holes. Rest easy; I'll be back quick."

Lund watched the tall man walk toward the dry stream bed. As if on instinct. He had said he was a stranger, but it was obvious that he knew country.

He wore buckskins and his face was hard as a dried hide stretched in the sun. He carried himself well, like a soldier. His shoulders were straight, wide. His back broad as a side of elk. He walked into it, but he walked out of it too. His mistake. He thought he was one of Staggs' men, but Staggs didn't know men like this one. There was something about Gunn that made him realize he wasn't an owlhooter, nor a poacher. He was hard and he probably could sling a gun, but he wasn't no ordinary man. He could have rode off and no one the wiser. But he was stickin' and he would carry him home, God willing. The only thing that bothered him about the stranger was his eyes. They were cold as iron and pale as a winter sky. And when they looked at you, they meant business; they hinted at many stories untold.

Gunn shook out his bandanna, gathered moss at the base of the bigger trees. From the north side. He looked for good dirt, spat on it, to keep it moist. He put the materials in the kerchief, found the stream bed. He dug down, found the water. On the banks, he gathered other herbs. He packed mud into the nest of leaves and moss and dry dirt. He made a sack of the bandanna. When he was finished, his bundle weighed near two pounds.

Lund looked in tough shape when Gunn returned. His face was drained of blood, his eyes closed. For a moment, Gunn thought he might be dead. He had made a sash from a ripped shirt, wrapped it around the man's wounds, but that wouldn't prevent any serious bleeding.

"Lund?"

Grandy's eyes opened. A trace of a smile creased his

13

face. The smile was wan.

Gunn's grey eyes flickered.

"It's going to hurt for a minute or two. A long minute or two."

"I know. It doesn't hurt much now."

Gunn almost frowned. This was not a good sign. The man might be closer to death than he knew.

"If I don't pack your wounds, you haven't a chance on that horse of mine. It's a good stretch up that mountain."

"You talk a hell of a lot to man what can't answer without feeling knives in his chest."

Gunn grinned, unfolded the bandanna.

He knelt down, looked into Lund's eyes.

"I'm going to turn you over on your side, get to your back first."

"Not a big hole, is it?"

"Not too big."

"You got any whiskey?"

"Seldom carry it. Sorry."

"I'll ask you kindly for a stick, or a bite on that Mex knife you carry on your belt."

Gunn's eyes narrowed, flickered with a pale light.

The knife was Mexican, given to him by a friend, for a favor. It was engraved with a legend that he lived by: No me saques sin razon, ni me guardes sin honor.

Don't draw me without reason, nor keep me without honor.

"You won't need a bite," said Gunn. "Just look at the blue sky and think about your daughters."

Gunn unwrapped the makeshift bandage. Lund winced a time or two, but did not pass out. Gently, Gunn rolled him over, began packing the back wound with the mud and the moss and the healing leaves. Lund groaned, but held on. The stomach wound was worse. Lund ground his teeth together as the stranger pushed the muddy concoction deep into the hole. When he was finished, Gunn wrapped the bandage around him as tenderly as he could.

"This will keep the bleeding down, maybe help you heal up," he said.

Lund looked up at him with glassy eyes.

"You lie like a damned nurse," he husked.

Gunn stood up, untied his horse, led him over to the wounded man.

"The tough part's just starting, Lund. Take my advice, you'll save your breath for the ride. You got a hole in you and I don't know what it hit or what it missed. I just know a forty-five ball tears pure hell out of a man—even if it hits him in the finger."

Lund said nothing. He drew a breath that would have been short for a healthy man and his eyes closed again as if he was wondering whether it was worth it or not to let the air back out. His face and lips took on a dull bluish cast before he choked, drew in more oxygen.

Gunn lifted him carefully, sat him in the saddle.

"Can you ride sitting up?" he asked. "I hate to drape you over the hindside of this horse the way you're breathing."

"Hurry. I hold on to you, I can ride behind you like a man."

Gunn swung up into the saddle. He stopped in the middle of the trail, picked up his Winchester, shoved it into its boot. Lund's arms were wrapped around him as Esquire jogged along at a slow gait.

It took the two men almost an hour to reach the top of the ridge. Gunn had to reach for him twice when his grip loosened and he almost fell from the horse. Gunn rode back of the cantle, after this happened the second time. He wrapped one arm around Lund to keep him from falling.

"Lund? We getting close?"

Lund's head raised; he opened his eyes.

"Just ahead. You done good, stranger." His voice was thick as if he had been drinking whiskey. "Two hunnert yards."

It was more like five hundred. But the cabin appeared in a clearing and Gunn began to breathe easier. Lund was almost a dead weight in his arm, and Esquire wearied under the extra weight, the steep climb.

A woman appeared on the porch, a rifle in her hand.

Gunn swallowed hard.

She was a savage-looking beauty, barefooted, blonde, fair-skinned, slender, wearing a loose dress that burst at the bodice as if her large breasts would break free at any moment.

A lazy curl of smoke drifted skyward from the cabin's stone chimney.

Gunn rode up on it without realizing how close he had been to it for the last fifty yards. Trees had been cut down around the cabin, but it was still hidden atop the ridge by the pines and spruce, the cedars.

"That it, Lund?"

Lund grunted in assent. He was hanging on, but his face was pasty, his eyes gilded with a dull coppery pain.

Gunn weaved Esquire through the stumps toward the porch. The house was quiet, looked empty.

Yet the smoke from the chimney said different.

The porch was wide, with wide steps. Which surprised Gunn. Chairs on the porch, pots of flowers hanging from the rafters. Someone gave a damn about how they lived, if not where they lived. The front door was closed. He saw a curtain move.

The door opened.

A barefoot, scantily-clad young woman padded on to the porch. The door creaked and another girl, younger, shyly stepped through it.

Gunn sucked in his breath.

They were beauties. Looked half-wild in the sun. Sun that wove through their hair, dazzled his eyes with reflections of spun gold, fine copper wire. Both were flame-haired, blue-eyed. Wide blue eyes, breasts struggling against the confinement of thin cloth.

"Pa!" exclaimed one of them, the youngest girl.

"Leni!" gasped Lund. "Kristina!"

Kristina, the eldest, left the porch in a leap that rivalled a gazelle's. She bounded gracefully down the steps.

"You're hurt, Pa," she breathed, her breasts fighting the skimpy cloth of her bodice. Gunn thought sure the material would tear and those two ripe melons would fall into view. They were symmetrical, the tops of them smooth and white as fresh cream. Mouthwatering. "It was Tolly Stagg, wasn't it?"

Leni followed her sister, cautiously, taking the steps gingerly, one at a time. Gunn thought she looked like a young fawn about to spook off the ridge. Her blue eyes were shadowed under thick dark lashes. Her eyes moved in their sockets, seeming to look everywhere at once. She appeared ready to bolt and run if she saw anything—anything at all.

"Pa, you—you've been shot? Is that blood from a bullet?" Kristina's hand touched her father's arm, her eyes remained fixed on his belly. "There's so much blood." Leni started weeping uncontrollably.

"Who's Stagg?" asked Gunn.

Kristina shot him an angry look.

"He says he's a miner. He's a damned thief. An outlaw; meaner than a Comanche dog."

Gunn let out a low whistle. There was fire in Kristina. Her eyes flashed like blue diamonds.

"Help me get Pa inside, Leni," said Kristina, dismissing Gunn with a withering look.

"I'll take him in," said Gunn.

Fresh blood soaked onto Lund's belly. It was bright red. Kristina's face drained of color. Gunn shoved her aside, helped Lund out of the saddle. Gunn sagged under the wounded man's full weight. Kristina and Leni both gasped when they saw their father's face contort in a pained grimace. Beads of sweat glistened on his forehead.

Kristina's face hardened into a mask of hatred.

"I'd like to twist the stones off the man who did this to you, Pa," she said bitterly.

Gunn hefted Lund in his arms, looked at her.

"I shot your pa," he said quietly.

CHAPTER THREE

Kristina looked at Gunn with a cold hatred.

"You lowdown bastard," she hissed.

Leni gasped. Her face drained of blood, chalked like a sandstone cliff in the bleak sun of a winter morning. She gaped at the tall man with the pale blue eyes that were almost colorless in the light. Her mouth tightened down into a crease across her comely face.

"You—you shot our pa?" she said, her words flat and lifeless as metal coins thudding onto a dry blanket. "Why?"

Gunn looked at her.

"Won't do much good to talk about it," he said. "You got a place for him to lie down?"

The women blinked, continued to glare at Gunn as if they could not believe he was there, was speaking to them. Kristina's teeth ground together, made a sound. She clenched her fists as it to strike the stranger who had admitted to shooting her father.

"You bastard," she seethed. "You terrible bastard."

Gunn saw that he was going to be in trouble unless he took charge. Both women were in shock. That was plain to see. They saw only one side of it. They were stone deaf and blind to boot.

"Look," he said, "let's get your pa to bed. He's in bad shape. May not have long to live. I shot him, but I didn't mean to kill him."

Leni's eyes opened wide. Her face whitened in horror

"You—you—" she blurted.

"Steady now, girl," Gunn said quietly. "Think."

He turned his back on the two women, eased Lund from the horse. Lund groaned and his daughters sucked in quick breaths. He sagged under the weight of the wounded man, held him steady as he could and started toward the porch.

Kristina was the first to recover her wits. She ran ahead of Gunn and opened the door for him. Leni followed, staring at her father, wringing her hands. Gunn stepped inside, his eyes adjusting for the change in light. The front room served as a place of comfort, with a large stuffed divan and chairs, a footstool, a couple of tables, a fireplace and hearth, framed Currier & Ives prints on the walls, vases with dried flowers and weeds artistically arranged, some doilies on the furniture, rifles and pistols hung on bare wall space.

"Follow me," said Kristina tautly. "I'll turn down Pa's bed. Leni, you fetch some water, get it to boiling."

Gunn laid Grandy on the bed. Kristina began pulling off his boots. Even though she tugged gently, Lund groaned. She winced every time he made a sound. Gunn loosened his belt, pulled his blood-soaked shirt away from the wound. The hole in Lund's belly was ugly, blue at the edges, turning yellowish in the surrounding area. Fresh blood seeped onto his belly, but at least it was not gushing. Still, Gunn figured that he must be bleeding inside and he was probably torn up pretty badly. A .44 slug showed little mercy for soft flesh.

"You ought to have a doc come out and look at that wound," Gunn told the girl.

"No," said Lund. "No doc. Waste of time anyway."

"Pa . . ."

"Hush, gal. You got to face facts. It don't hurt no more and that's a bad sign. At first it burned like fire and then it made me real sick. But now I feel right peaceful. You get me comfortable and let me spend my last moments with you and Leni. That's all I ask." Lund's eyes glazed over with fresh tears but he bit off the sudden spasm of pain that racked his body. Sweat oozed out of the pores on his forehead. Kristina got the boots off, stood near her father's head, held his hand gently.

"Pa, maybe you aren't hurt so bad as you think. I can get some herbs and some of that blue clay up at the spring. Leni could get some medicants in town and be back by morning."

"I got a lot to say," the dying man said grimly. "Go get your sister quick."

Kristina shot Gunn a lot of helplessness, but her eyes laid blame on him. He said nothing, but stood there wondering how long Lund could last. The man was bleeding inside and there was no way to stop it. Herbs and clay would not help him now.

Kristina went to get Leni. Gunn and Lund were alone.

"I don't have much time, feller."

"No."

"I made a bad mistake."

"Yeah," Gunn admitted.

"What about you? You got plans? You need to be anywhere in particular?"

"No, I reckon not. What're you driving at Lund?"

"There's game here, a business I got started. You're a pretty fair shot. Like you to consider working out the season, long enough to fill out my contracts. I'll give the business to you if you'll take care of my daughters, see to it they get settled proper down to Denver."

Gunn did not want to give Lund an answer now. He didn't have to, for Leni and Kristina returned at that moment. Leni's eyes were red-rimmed from crying. She had on an apron now and her hands were wet.

"Pa, please don't die," wailed Leni, rushing to her father's bedside. "I love you so much."

"Now, now daughter, don't cry. I got things to tell you and your sister. I want Gunn to stay here and listen."

Kristina plainly disapproved. She gave Gunn a look that left no doubt in his mind.

"Pa, this man shot you, maybe killed you," she said. "How can you . . . ?"

"Warn't his fault. I take the blame," said Lund. "Might have been the other way around and then I'd have that on my conscience. You just listen to what I got to say. Hear?"

"Yes, Pa," both women chorused obediently.

"Now, we ain't got no friends up here. That's my own damned fault too. Ever since your mother . . . but that don't count now. I want you girls to pack up, go to Denver. I got a little money put by for you. You look in the strongbox I keep under the rug in the front room. There's enough to tide you over until you both find yourselves husbands. Gunn here can finish up my contracts and take out his share if he wants. They can get their owned damned meat next year."

The talking was an effort for Lund. His breathing came hard now. His head sank into the pillow. Leni took his hand, almost recoiled when she felt how cold it was. Kristina touched his wrist, fought back tears.

"Pa, we can do it ourselves," she said. "We don't need any help from this man."

Lund did not reply. He licked dry lips, wheezed.

"Please leave us alone with our pa," Kristina said to Gunn. Leni shot her sister a dark look, bit her lip. Gunn nodded, left the room. He walked through the kitchen, to the back, opened the door. He stepped out on the porch, fished out the makings. The scent of pine was strong in the air. So, also was the smell of urine, horse droppings.

The corral was small, but it had a shelter, a tack room. There was a wagon on the other side of the corral, big enough to haul hides or meat. A smaller wagon, probably used for hauling supplies in from town, stood, its tongue drooping, in the middle of a cluster of trees. Gunn finished rolling his quirly, licked its tip, stuck it in his mouth. He found a match, struck it. He drew deeply on the cigarette, walked off the porch toward the corral. There were three horses nibbling on grain, dried grass. Prairie grass, he thought, bluestem. Harvested from God knows where. The horses were fat, well cared for, heavy duty animals that could haul a load over steep mountain trails.

He stood there, smoking, wondering what he should do. Lund wouldn't last the night. He was supposed to meet a friend in Oro City sometime in the next week or so. Jed Randall, coming down from Wyoming after a trip to find out the beef situation. Gunn knew the answer. Wyoming wouldn't need any beef. They had plenty of their own. The big cattle drives had seen their day. People were settling the West, the towns were swelling up with people, homesteaders fanned out into the foothills, took up empty space on the prairies, built their sod huts and dug in like doodlebugs, began planting crops and putting up fences of stone and wood. Cheyenne was choked with people, not all of them reputable. The town was getting a nasty name and Gunn wasn't surprised. Colorado was booming now that the Utes and the Arapahoes had been cleaned out.

He didn't hear the back door open nor the soft footsteps padding his way. He was lost in reverie, wondering if he should let Lund die in peace, give his regrets to the girls in advance and just ride on into Oro City and get blind staggering drunk.

"Mister Gunn?"

Startled, Gunn almost dropped his cigarette. As it was, he burned his finger getting it out of his mouth. His right hand curled around the butt of his Colt. He turned, saw Leni standing there, a look of surprise on her face.

"Were you going to shoot me, too?" she asked. Her voice had the melody of tinkling bells in it.

"You give a man a start, sneakin' up on him like that."

His face reddened and he drew his right hand away

from his pistol, stuck the cigarette back in his mouth. The smoke curled up to his nostrils, to his grey-blue eyes.

"I'm sorry. Kristina is talking to Pa and I wanted to ask you if you were going to stay here with us like he wants you to."

"Should I? Your sister doesn't like me much. You neither probably."

"I like you," she said. "I know you didn't mean to shoot Pa. At least I don't think you did. He says it was his fault."

"He's dying from that mistake. I don't blame your sis any. I'd feel the same."

"Give her a little time to get over the shock. Then you can talk to her. We're gonna miss Pa a lot. I—I don't know what we're gonna do."

She broke down, then, began sobbing. She rushed up to Gunn, fell into his arms. This time, he dropped the cigarette. He held her against him while she wept, not knowing what to say. Leni was just a kid. It was tough on her. He didn't know what they were going to do either. Lund should have thought some things out in advance. It was plain he hadn't.

The back door banged open.

Kristina stood there, looking at her sister in Gunn's arms. She could not hear the sobbing sounds. Instead, she saw only that Gunn was embracing her younger sister.

"Leni! Get away from that man!" she shouted.

Gunn looked up, saw her. He patted Leni's head, released her. Leni turned, then, her face streaked with tears.

"Kristina—you're so heartless sometimes."

25

Leni shot Gunn a look of sympathy, then ran around the cabin to the front. Kristina walked down the steps toward Gunn. She stopped a few feet from him and glared at him defiantly.

"Just what do you think you're doing, mister?" she asked.

"Minding my own business, for one thing."

"Are you? It looks to me like you're butting in where you don't belong. Haven't you done enough damage for one day? I don't like seeing your filthy hands on my sister. She may not know the difference, but I do. You think because my pa is disabled that we're defenseless. Well, we're not. If you're not out of here in five minutes, I'm going to shoot you."

"Do you always jump to conclusions, Miss?"

"I know your kind, Gunn. That probably isn't even your real name. You're a saddletramp, a drifter, preying on good honest folks. You probably came here to get in on the silver boom, like all the rest of those drunken dreamers in Oro City. You shoot our pa and then think you can have your way with us. I still think you're one of Tolly Stagg's bunch. I wouldn't put it past him to hire the likes of you."

Her blue eyes scorched Gunn's face. Her blonde hair glinted with sunlight, but her beauty had turned savage. Gunn knew that if she wasn't handled right, she'd make good on her threats. There was bound to be trouble here. More when Lund died. He didn't want any part of it. Still, he felt responsible for putting Lund down, even though it hadn't been his fault. His instincts were still strongly telling him to ride on, to leave this trouble before there was more tragedy to confront them.

"I don't work for Staggs. Never heard of him. But I'll get out of your hair, ma'am. I thought I could help, but it's plain you've got something stuck in your craw and no amount of swallowing's going to help."

Kristina's eyes flared with anger.

"I don't need your insults."

"Nor I yours," Gunn said.

He started to walk away, but Kristina blocked his path.

"And keep away from Leni!" she growled.

Gunn grabbed her upraised wrists, felt her struggle. He thought she had been going to strike him and now he was sure of it. He held her firmly, trying not to hurt her.

"Lady, you got a lot to learn about men."

"And I suppose you think you're going to teach me?"

"I might if you don't settle down. I'll say goodbye to your pa and be on my way. Far as I'm concerned, you deserve anything you get from here on out."

Gunn fought against his rising anger. Kristina was overwrought, he knew. But she was too quick with her temper. She needed a good slap in the face. For a minute, he was tempted. Mighty tempted.

They glared at each other for several seconds. Gunn's jaw hardened. He felt her wrists begin to tremble. Her breasts rose with a deep sucked-in breath. He smiled coolly at her and released the pressure.

"You bastard," she husked.

"Yes ma'am," he grinned.

That's when they both froze. Leni's scream curdled their blood, a scream that came from within the house. She screamed again, a terrible, wrenching scream that was full of agony and despair.

Gunn was the first inside, Kristina a few paces behind him. He found Leni standing by her father's bed, sobbing, shaking uncontrollably.

"Oh pa," she muttered, "please don't die."

Grandy's face was ashen. He didn't appear to be breathing. Gunn felt the large vein in his neck, searching for a pulse. There was none. He bent over, put his ear to Lund's mouth. He could not detect a breath.

"What happened?" asked Kristina, stunned.

"He—he just made a funny sound in his throat, tried to sit up and then he—he fell back down and started gasping for breath." Leni's eyes rolled wildly in their sockets. She was scared.

Gunn looked at Kristina, shook his head.

"Is he—is he dead?" she asked.

"He's dead," said Gunn.

Kristina dipped her head, then raised it. Her eyes moistened, but she did not weep.

"I—I'll take care of him," she said quietly. "Leni, I'll need hot water, some towels and a washcloth. I'll fix pa up good."

"Yes, Kristina." Leni threw herself on her father, hugged his lifeless body. Then she stood up, walked numbly from the room.

"I'll help you bury him," Gunn said. "Any place in particular?"

"There's a stand of aspen he always liked," she said, her voice dreamlike and soft. "Up the slope a ways. There's a spring and a flat place. The ground should be soft. We don't use that water. It's just a small spring, no more than a trickle. It's quiet up there and he always sat on a stump just to get away from things, do some thinking. I think he'll like it there. I appreciate your help, Mister Gunn. You can stay for supper. I guess Pa wouldn't want me to be inhospitable, would you, Pa?"

She cried then, and Gunn put his arms around her. She did not resist. He was glad she had wept. He knew she was on the verge of hysteria. The shock had been hard. Lund's face was waxen now and he was starting to stiffen up. He let loose of Kristina, strode to the door. He stopped, looked at her. She turned to face him.

"If you need me, I'll be up there. I'm sorry, ma'am."

Kristina sucked in a breath.

"I—I know you are. I misjudged you, Gunn. Will you forgive me?"

"Nothing to forgive," he said, and then he was gone.

The cabin began to fill up with sadness.

CHAPTER FOUR

Gunn found a shovel in the tackroom. He hiked up the slope, found the grove of quaking aspen. Their white trunks shimmered in the sunlight. There was a stump, just large enough for a man to sit on, and a trickle of water from a shelf of shaley rocks. The stump was worn on top; there were footprints around it. From there, he could see over the cabin, over the vast forests, the distant peaks. It was a good spot.

There was a level spot in the open but among the aspens. Their leaves whispered from the breeze as he dug the grave that would hold Grandy Lund's corpse. He threw his hat over by the stump, began marking out a grave. He dug until he began to sweat. Then he removed his shirt and continued deepening and widening the grave. The ground was soft and there were few stones in that place. There were columbines growing there and he heard a jay blistering the air with invective. A pair of crows flew over and he saw a lone buzzard circling high above, riding the air currents as if it had already detected the first faint aroma of death.

They buried Grandy Lund at dusk.

Kristina and Leni had dressed him in his one suit,

which was all shiny from wear. She had put color on his cheeks with rouge, combed his hair. Before Gunn put him in the grave, he closed over the winding sheet. The girls sobbed and held on to each other for comfort.

"Would you say a prayer, Mister Gunn?" asked Kristina.

"I don't hardly know what to say," he said.

"Just say a few words. Whatever you feel."

"Yes'm."

Gunn had never spoken words over a man's grave before. Not out loud. He had grieved at his wife Laurie's grave and could not even remember what words had been spoken. But he knew it was proper and probably proper that he say something, not for Lund's sake, but to comfort his grieving daughters.

He held his hat in his hands, looked down at the sheeted body in the hole. Then he looked up at the sky, closed his eyes.

"Heavenly Father, we bury this good man who is now in your keep. We are sorry he had to leave this life, but we know you have a better one waiting for him. Watch over his daughters and forgive me for having a hand in this against my will. Thanks for listening to our prayers, Father. Goodbye Grandy Lund. I hope we meet again, bye and bye."

Gunn stood there, his eyes closed, listening to the girls sob. Then he heard them walk away, down the slope toward the cabin. He put on his hat, picked up the shovel. He began filling the grave, his sweat clammy on his flesh. The sun was going down and a man was buried. It grew quiet, except for the soft shoosh of dirt striking dirt. The sheet disappeared from view and the grave filled up. He mounded it off neatly, then worked loosed a flat piece of shale, sandstone, he figured, and tamped it in the ground for a temporary headstone. He thought he was alone, but the women came back, carrying fresh-cut columbines in their arms. They placed them on the grave, kneeling to do so. They looked very pretty in their summer dresses, their bonnets. He waited until they were finished, and then walked with them down the path, the shovel unobtrusively tucked under his arm. He dropped it off at the tackroom as the ladies went on inside the house. He did not go in for a long time, but built a cigarette, smoked it.

He felt empty inside. Grandy's death bothered him a lot. A man could not afford to make too many mistakes in the West. Lund must have been pushed to his limit to have made one this serious. Tolly Stagg. The name hadn't meant anything before, but it did now. Stagg had something to answer for now. No court could convict him. But this went beyond that. If he, Gunn, stayed on, he would run into Stagg. It would be a fresh deck, a fresh deal.

Gunn let the smoke calm him. The sky turned golden, then purple, with slashes of pink and silver etching the horizon, tinging the few cloud puffs high in the sky.

He did not hear Kristina come up behind him.

"A penny for your thoughts," she said softly. "Were you thinking about Pa?"

"In a way. I was thinking about Stagg. I might look him up one of these days."

"I don't want to talk about him now, but I'm glad. I was wrong. I know where the blame lies now. Won't you come in for supper? It's not much, but it'll stick to your ribs. We'll have coffee and talk later on, if you like."

He put out his cigarette, looked at her. She had changed from the frock she had worn before, the bonnet was gone. She wore a simple dress, with a black mourning band around the sleeve. But there was a flower in her hair, a blue columbine that matched her eyes.

"Yes," he told her, "I'd like to talk with you and Leni. She all right?"

"She's fine." Kristina paused, then took Gunn's arm, began to lead him toward the house. "I'm glad you're here. It helps."

Gunn started to get up from the table. Kristina reached out a hand, touched his arm.

"Don't get up. Leni will clear the plates and I'll help her wash the dishes later. She'll want to hear this."

"The meal was fine, ma'am. I don't mind helping. . . ."

"Nonsense, Mister Gunn. You're our guest. Leni, would you bring some of Pa's brandy and a cigar for the gentleman?"

"I'd be pleasured," said Leni, her brown eyes shining. "Won't be but a minute."

Gunn rubbed his belly. It had been a fine meal. Better than any he'd had in a long time. Good beef, potatoes, hot biscuits, clover honey, a dish of pears and cream. The tea had been hot and strong, took away the weariness. And, now, brandy sounded good. He wouldn't mind the cigar either. Neither Leni nor

Kristina had said much about their father during supper and they didn't talk about old times. Usually people would remember good times they had with the loved one who had passed away. But there was a lingering sadness over the table, despite the light-hearted banter of the women. Gunn didn't know what to make of it. He felt like an intruder in a dead man's house. But he had no doubt that he was welcome, if only to fill up an emptiness.

Leni, especially, had been attentive during the meal, waiting on him hand and foot, solicitous of his every need. Kristina had been more reserved, but polite enough. Mainly, they had tried to find out a lot about him. He hadn't told them much. Just that his name was really William Gunnison, he had fought in the War between the States, had been married, his wife had died. He didn't tell them how. They'd had enough of violence for one day. He told them that he had shortened his name to Gunn for private reasons. Now he sensed that Kristina had something to say to him. Something important. They had stuffed him like a fatted calf and now they were both ready to exact something from him. What, he did not know. He scraped his boots on the floor, stretched out his legs. He had taken a bath, shaved, gotten most of the grime out from under his fingernails.

"Here you are, Mister Gunn," said Leni, bringing a dusty bottle of brandy and a humidor full of cigars. The lid was open. He took a cigar, smelled it. Fresh.

"Bring us two glasses," said Kristina, "and a match for Mister Gunn."

"It's just Gunn," he said, for perhaps the tenth time. "No mister in front of it. Besides, it makes me feel old."

34

Both women laughed and it sounded good. Leni brought three glasses. Kristina gave her a sharp look, then weakened.

"Not too much, Leni. You know how you get with brandy."

Leni giggled, poured the brandy. All three glasses held the same amount. Another sharp look from Kristina.

"Don't worry. I can handle it," said Leni. "This late at night it'll only make me sleepy." She began clearing away the dishes. Every so often, she'd stop, take a sip of brandy. Gunn swallowed some and it went down smoothly. Kristina hardly touched her own glass.

"Well, Gunn, we asked you a lot of questions, but we didn't tell you much about ourselves. I guess we didn't fully trust you. But Pa did. He told me while you were outside that he knew of you, of the trouble you had up on the Cache de la Poudre a few years back. Your wife was murdered, raped, and you went after those responsible. He said you had a big reputation, but were not a bad man. He thought you might be the kind of man who would want to stick around, help us. I fought against it, but now I'm not sure that he wasn't right."

"He was right!" blurted Leni, clattering a dish into the basin on the sinkboard.

"Hush, let me finish, Leni."

Gunn picked up a taper Leni had left on the table, bit the end off the cigar, picked it out of his teeth and set it on a saucer. He lit the cigar, let the smoke filter through his nose, tickle his throat. It was a good cigar, strong and sweet-smelling like rain-soaked wood.

"Your pa used to making snap judgments?" asked Gunn.

"He is — uh, was. Yes. Our mother died seven years ago. She was killed by Utes. We, too, had a home, a little ranch. Pa brought us up into the mountains after that. To hide."

"From the Utes? Heck, they were driven . . ."

"Not from the Utes, Gunn," said Kristina, leaning over the table, "from civilization. From men. His neighbors wouldn't help when the farm was burned. The Indians raped our mother, mutilated her. He tried to get help. The smoke could be seen for miles. Everyone was afraid of the Utes. They remembered Meeker and they were scared, but Pa didn't care. If they had come to help they could have saved our mother. She'd be alive today. Yes, I'm bitter. Pa became a recluse. He hated all mankind. But he needed money for us, so he chose the best job he could get, the one that would give him the least contact with men. He became a hunter, only going to town to sell his meat, his hides. The rest of the time, he lived up here with us. And, he was all we had. Oh, he'd take us into town once in a while, but we felt like prisoners. He watched over us like a hawk."

"I see," said Gunn. Her story explained a lot of things. Lund was little more than a hermit. It looked as if some of his habits had rubbed off on his daughters. They were little more than half-wild, pretending to be civilized, but they really lacked refinement. They had character, though, and for him that would be enough to get them by.

"You can go to Oro City and mine silver," Kristina said, "if that's your intention. But you'll go bust. Like Pa did once. He tried it. Mining was pretty solitary, too. Then he found out that the only people making money were those who sold goods to the miners. The miners came and went, but the tradesmen are still there, many of them rich. He hunted food for those crazy miners and he provided for us pretty well. I figure Leni and I can fulfill the contracts he made and we'll do all right."

"Hard for a woman to hunt and skin big game. You have to know the game trails, the habits of deer and elk."

"We can do it," said Kristina defiantly.

Gunn wanted to laugh. But he couldn't embarrass these two women. Kristina had talked all around it, but he knew what she was leading up to. Lund had wanted him to stay on. The contracts, his word, meant a lot to him, even while he was dying. He could see that it meant a lot to Kristina, too. As he looked at her, she picked up her brandy glass, downed it. Her eyes misted and she gasped for breath.

"That's pretty strong stuff to take at one gulp," he said.

"I'm very nervous. This is hard for me to talk about," she said curtly, her eyes wide.

Gunn drew on his cigar, sipped more brandy. He had given it some thought. He couldn't just leave them here. They couldn't hunt. Despite his faults, it was obvious that Grandy Lund had raised his daughters to be ladies, not mountain women tracking big game. The Rockies were merciless. It was hard hunting uphill half the time. It was a young man's job, not a woman's. He knew the mountains. Lund, apparently did too. Or he wouldn't have survived all these years. But it took time to know them and the women didn't have time.

Leni finished stacking the dishes, sat down. She sipped her brandy, eyes fluttering to hide the burning in her stomach. Kristina fanned herself with a napkin, although it was not warm. They waited for him to say something. When he was ready, he spoke.

"I don't want to run out on you," he said, "but I don't want to take advantage of you either. I'm not a nursemaid, but I feel responsible for your situation. What I have to propose to you is a straight business proposition. Now, your pa has contracts to supply wild game meats to the miners. I'll buy up those contracts, fill 'em out, pay you and your sister a fair share for helping me. Or you can sell 'em outright and go to Denver like your pa wants. Whatever you want. Either way, you'll have some cash and be out from under."

"We couldn't run out of our obligations," said Kristina. "Why don't you just work for us? We'll pay you a fair salary."

"Because that would be buying more trouble with Stagg. If I buy up the contracts, he'll have to come after me. I want him. I want him bad."

"Do you mind if Leni and I talk this over? We'll give you our answer in the morning."

"Suit yourself? Can I have a taste more of that brandy? Then I'll throw my bedroll in the barn and sleep out there."

"Leni, pour Gunn some more brandy. But you'll not sleep in the barn. I take back what I said about you being a saddletramp. Pa would want you to have his room. I'll fix it up for you."

Before Gunn could reply, Kristina was off to Lund's bedroom. Leni poured her glass and Gunn's with a generous amount of brandy. She sipped hers as she sat down beside him.

"I'm glad you're staying, Gunn," she said in that musical voice of hers. Her dark eyes flashed with promise. "I'll get Kristina to take up your offer."

"You'd better lighten up on that brandy, hadn't you?"

Leni giggled. She batted her eyes at Gunn and he felt an odd, unexpected tug at his loins.

"I'll be just fine," she said.

"What did your sister mean about you having too much brandy?"

"Oh," she said coyly, "you'll find out. One of these days. I'm not going to tell."

Gunn finished his cigar, suddenly feeling very uncomfortable. Leni's eyes locked on him, wouldn't turn him loose. He felt as if she was stripping him naked. Then, he felt her leg press against his, under the table. He moved his away, but she touched him again, moved her chair closer. He drank his brandy neat. He felt her hand on his leg, squeezing it.

"Leni, you don't want to start anything," he said.

"Oh, don't be such a prude. I'll bet you know lots of girls."

Her hand went up his leg, into his crotch.

"Few as bold as you, young lady."

"Mmm. I bet you're getting hard, aren't you?"

He was getting hard. But he didn't like her teasing him like that. He reached under the table, grabbed her wrist. He moved her hand out of his lap.

"Leni!" called Kristina from the bedroom. "Come here. I need you."

Gunn let out a sigh of relief.

Leni got up from the table, kissed him quickly on the cheek, whispered into his ear.

39

"I want you," she breathed, and then danced away before he could reply. Her voice had made the hackles rise on the back of his neck. His skin tingled. His cheek was warm where she had kissed him.

And, he was bone hard.

"Damn," he muttered, "what in hell have I got myself into now?"

CHAPTER FIVE

Gunn closed the door to Lund's room, put a chair against it. He wished it had a lock, but the chair would have to do. He was tired. The room smelled of soap and perfume. The women had cleaned it up, put fresh sheets on the bed. He didn't mind sleeping in a dead man's room. But he didn't know what to make of Leni. She had come on pretty bold and he didn't want any trouble with Kristina. If she accepted his offer, he could buy the outfit, flush Stagg out in the open and fill out Lund's contracts. That way no one could accuse him of taking advantage of the situation or of the daughters. When he had finished up, he could sell out, send the women their share of the proceeds.

He shucked his boots, let them hit the floor loudly. He could hear dishes clattering in the kitchen, an occasional giggle, followed by a loud command to hush. Each person handled grief in his or her own way. Some people got the giggles, others got morose. The women were strong. The full impact probably hadn't hit them yet. His presence had guaranteed that they'd be kept busy, preoccupied. They handled it well, he thought. From what he gathered, Lund had kept a tight rein on his daughters. Maybe that was why Leni had acted the way she had. That, and the brandy. She'd get over it. She'd probably pass out, wouldn't even remember what she had done in the morning. Sometimes people acted a little crazy after they had lost a loved one. He had. He had gone looking for men and killed them, one by one. Until he found out his wife's real killer. The shock had been great. Now, finally, all those responsible were dead. But he had been crazy, all right. Plumb crazy.

He hung his gunbelt on the bedpost, slid out of his clothes. He opened the window, let the fresh night air in, the pine scent. It was quiet. He blew out the lamp, eased into the bed, pushed the covers down. He wouldn't need them until morning. He let the air wash over him, closed his eyes. He tried not to think of Lund and the morning's trouble. He tried to think of other things. But Leni's face kept appearing and he felt her kiss on his cheek, the whispered phrase rang again in his ears.

He tossed and turned until finally he no longer heard voices and the rattle of dishes. The weariness overtook him and he fell into a deep sleep.

Leni waited until she was certain that Kristina was asleep. It had seemed like hours since they had gone to bed. Kristina had been too tired to talk. Now, Leni rose from her bed, tiptoed across the room. Kristina, on the other bunk, didn't stir.

Leni slipped through the door, down the hall. She was hot. All over. She couldn't get Gunn out of her mind. The brandy had made her bold, but she wanted him long before that. Out at the corral she had felt the first stirrings of desire. The brandy had

42

helped, but that had long since worn off. She couldn't sleep until she touched him again, kissed him. He hadn't turned her down, actually. He had just mildly rebuffed her. Probably because Kristina had been around. But she wanted him now. She didn't care what the consequences might be. He was a man and she was a starving woman. Her loins ached for him and she might never have a better opportunity.

She stopped in front of the door to her father's room, hesitant. Her father's room! How terrible of her! He had died only hours before and now she was about to enter it and do something he would not approve of if he were alive! Did she dare? Would Kristina ever forgive her if she found out? She put her hand on the latch, wondering if she could, or should, go through with it. Would Gunn think she was terrible, coming to his bed like this, half-naked, wearing only a thin gown, nothing on underneath?

Her heart beat wildly in her chest. She lifted the latch, pushed on the door. It didn't move! She pushed again. Something was blocking the door! She didn't dare force it. She would make too much noise. Kristina would hear. She would wake Gunn up and he'd probably tell her to go back to bed!

A sudden anger gripped her. How dare he lock her out? This was more her house than his! She tried the door again. Solid. For a moment she considered the foolishness of her actions. She started back toward her bedroom, then paused. No, she wasn't going to let this stop her. She wanted Gunn, even if for only a few moments. Just to lie with him, touch him, kiss him. Make him want her as she wanted him.

An idea occurred to her. Perhaps she could go in

his room another way. She tiptoed to the kitchen, feeling her way in the dark. She bumped against the table where they had supped. Something tinkled. The brandy bottle and the glasses were still on the table. She had forgotten to put them away. She groped for the bottle, found it. It was uncorked. She tipped the bottle up to her mouth, swallowed some of the brandy. It burned her throat, warmed her belly. She felt bold and determined now.

She went out the back door, leaving it slightly ajar. She listened to see if Kristina had awakened. It was quiet. Stars sprinkled the sky and there was a mild breeze blowing. She made her way around the side of the cabin, to her father's window. It was open. The curtains fluttered like ghosts. She jumped up, grabbed the sill. Her bare feet found footholds on the logs. She pulled herself up, hauled herself over the window. She hung there, her heart pounding, her legs outside, her breasts and torso inside. She squirmed over the sill, slid headfirst onto the floor. She braced herself with her hands, then brought her legs all the way inside. She crouched there for a moment, getting her bearings.

Gunn was asleep. He snored quietly. She saw his bulk mounded on the bed, a dark shape atop the sheets. She got to her feet, crept toward the bed. He was on the opposite side. There was room for her. She drew a deep breath, tried to still the rumble of her heart. She was sure that the noise was filling the room.

She lay beside him, controlling her breath. She felt like giggling. She had made it! Gunn did not know she was there. He lay on his back, a pair of shorts his only clothing. The shorts were dark, loose. She snuggled close to him, smelled his sweaty man's scent. Her senses sharpened, tingled. She reached out a hand, touched his crotch. He was soft. Her loins twitched with desire, as she slid her hand carefully and slowly inside his shorts. She touched soft flesh. Her fingers burned. She closed them around the limp organ. She had done this only once before in her life—in Oro City, at the livery, with a stableboy. She had touched his cock and made it hard. That was after drinking the brandy that time. Kristina had found her just as the boy was reaching under her dress. Kristina had pulled her ear and slapped them. The boy had run off, the coward, but she had never forgotten that sensation, that awesome feeling of making him hard.

She stroked Gunn's cock, kneaded it in her hand. Just as she had done with the stableboy. She felt it grow warm. Then, it began to harden. A sudden thrill raced through her veins. This time, Kristina wouldn't stop her!

Gunn basked in the deepest layers of sleep. He dreamed he was on a desert and the sun was hot. He was afoot and the sands were thick. He was looking for water. His throat was cracked and dry. He saw a lake in the distance and the lake drew closer without any effort on his part. He came up to it and fell in. The waters were warm. There were fish swimming in it and snakes. Something brushed against his leg. He grew terrified. Something wrapped around his loins, was trying to swallow his manhood. The lake disappeared and he was in a room with an unknown woman. She was naked. He was hard and wanted her. She touched him, squeezed his cock. He tried to force

45

her down, spread her legs. She slithered away and his cock grew larger and larger until its weight was too much to bear. The woman's face kept changing. She was laughing at him.

Gunn awoke with a start, shaking off sleep.

"Huh?" he said. The room was dark, but something was in bed with him. He reached out, touched a piece of cloth. Then he felt a hand squeeze his manhood.

"Gunn, I still want you." That musical voice, whispering close to his ear.

"Leni? Have you gone plumb loco?"

"Shhh! Just let me touch you." Her hand squeezed him. Gunn felt desire flood his loins.

"I told you not to start anything," he said.

"I wanted to."

"You have to finish it then."

"I know. I want to. I'm hot, Gunn, real hot."

"You're just a kid."

"I'm old enough."

"You're loco, dammit."

She giggled quietly in the dark, ringed his neck with a bare arm. He smelled the heady scent of brandy on her breath as she leaned to kiss him. She found his lips with hers, pressed hard. Her tongue slithered into his mouth. An electric jolt surged through his spinal cord. Suddenly, Leni was no longer a little girl, but a young woman. He kissed her hungrily, probing her moist warm mouth with his tongue. She had started something all right, something that he would damned sure finish.

He grabbed her roughly, drew her to him. Her one hand held on to his manhood, squeezing it as its veins swelled with blood.

46

"Get out of that gown," he gruffed, kissing her savagely.

"Yes, yes," she husked.

He ripped his shorts from his lean frame as Leni stretched, slipped her thin gown over her head. He saw her silhouetted by the window, her form faintly starlit. Her breasts were jaunty, firm in profile. Her hair cascaded back down her neck as she tossed the gown to the floor. She fell into his arms and he grabbed her, pulled her hard against him. They kissed, their passions explosive now that they were naked. He felt her soft breasts mash against his chest. She stroked the hard muscles of his arms, squirmed her loins against his thighs.

He pressed her down to the bed, touched one of her breasts. It was soft, yielding. He teased the nipple with his finger. It grew hard as a gumdrop. Her hand found him again, squeezed his cock with a caressing pressure.

"I—I've wanted this," she breathed. "Don't stop, Gunn, don't stop."

"Let's hope your big sister doesn't walk in her sleep."

"Don't even say that!"

"You'd be better be ready then. You keep touching me like that you're going to have your hands full of seed."

"No! Don't do that! Don't cheat me."

He laughed a low dry laugh, buried his face between her breasts. He began tonguing her nipples while she rubbed his thighs frantically, touching his scrotum, his penis as if trying to possess them. She arched her back and moaned as he suckled her teats, laving their rubbery thumblets with his tongue. Her body thrashed on the bed and he knew she was going to be a tigress. There was much to her body, and all of it was good. There wasn't an ounce of fat on her, but she was fullblown, buxom. He touched between her legs, felt the dampness, the wiry thatch that covered the portals of her sex. She bucked, wriggled as if seized by a sudden spasm.

She cried out and begged him to take her. He could not understand the words, but he knew the tone, the throaty sound a woman makes when she wants to be loved. He rose up above her, pried her legs apart with his knees. She shivered as he came close. Her hands slid around his neck, dovetailed. He moved between her legs, his swollen organ throbbing, poised.

He found her nest easily. With a gentle nudge, he pushed inside her, past her swollen lips. She made a sound in her throat. Her fingers tightened on his neck. He sank into her, into the bubbly mass of steaming flesh. His cock slid across her clitoris, jolting her. Her body thrashed as he sank still deeper until his manhood was bathed in the hot juices that drenched her tunnel.

"Oh, Gunn, it—it's so good," she stammered. "I—I didn't know it would be this good."

He sank still deeper, but knew before he struck the hymen that she was a virgin. Whatever had driven her to him was certainly not based on experience, but on wishing. Her maidenhead was like leather, tough as a boot. He could sink no farther until he slashed it away, rammed through the membrane.

"You might hurt some," he told her.

"I hurt now. All over. And it feels good. Just don't

48

stop, Gunn. I think I had one of those climber things."

"Climax," said Gunn drily.

"Yes, one of those. I felt like lightning hit me and all shivery inside."

"Likely, that's what you had. I'll try not to hurt you much."

"My cherry's in there, huh? Oh, I've heard the boys talk and tease. Is that what you call it?"

"Sometimes. A maidenhead's what your ma probably called it."

"She never talked about such things. Kristina didn't neither. She kept putting it off until I grew up."

"Well, you're about to grow up quick, Leni. Just hang on."

He plumbed her slowly, in and out, drawing his hard slicksmooth cock over her trigger until she was bucking like a bronc with a burr under its saddle. She wept and screamed, softly screamed, every time he ticked off the trigger. Her arms wrapped around his torso and he could feel her fingers scratching at his flesh like the claws of a crawdad, pinching him, raking his ribs. He kept hammering at the maidenhead, weakening it with every thrust.

It was hard to keep from exploding his seed. She was a tigress. Her legs went out of control as she orgasmed, flying up into the air, getting him in a scissorlock as if they were wrestlers in a dark arena.

He pounded the maidenhead, felt it weaken. Leni was frantic now, wanting to pull him in all the way. And he could stand it no longer. He rose up, jerked his cock clear to the mouth of her pussy and then plunged deep and hard.

"That's it, Gunn, fuck me hard!"

He rammed through the hymen, ripping it to shreds. She twitched slightly and clawed his back. But he went through and poked to the deepest part of her, into virgin flesh, into a boiling cauldron where no man had gone before. Her whole body quivered as he lingered there, trying to keep from spewing his milk. He let his mind drift away, let her spasms pass while he calmed his seething lust for a few more moments of mutual pleasure.

Her body, as his, was slick with sweat. He kissed her on the forehead, tenderly, tasted the salty moisture. She kissed his lips, caressed his torso with exploring hands.

"It didn't hurt," she said. "Not much. Just like a cut on the finger when you get salt in it. It—it felt wonderful. I like you in deep like this. I want you to stay there."

"Leni, we've both made a lot of noise. Your sister's not a stone."

"She sleeps right sound."

"Don't count on it. You just let me finish up and then you scoot back to your own bed."

"I—I couldn't bear to leave you after this."

"You'd better, if you ever want me again. Do it my way this time. Dammit, Leni, you ought to be spanked."

"You can do anything you want to me," she said and the music was in her voice again like faroff cowbells.

He said nothing, but began stroking her again. He brought her up to high pitch again, fucked her until she was breathless, a clawing, thrashing mass of flesh.

And then he rammed clear to the puckered mouth of her womb and let his seed shoot free, let the electricity race through him until he was mindless, spent, full of her and the mystery of their coupling.

He quivered against her, his penis spewing out the last of the seed from his scrotum. She held him tightly, mashing her breasts against his chest.

It was over.

"Gunn, did I make you happy?"

"Yes." He pulled free of her, lay on his back, panting.

"You have to wait a long time to be able to do it again, don't you? I heard that."

"You heard a lot of things. Pieces of things. You never heard it all."

"No. I know that. Don't be mad at me."

"I'm not mad at you. But you have to go. We can talk about this some other time."

"Do I have to go just yet. It makes me feel like you don't want me anymore, like you're throwing me away."

He sighed, rose up on one elbow, looked down at her.

"There you go again, talking about things you heard about, Leni. Just get those notions out of your head. Just . . ."

He never finished.

They both stiffened when they heard Kristina's voice through the door.

"Leni? Leni? Where are you?"

"Move," whispered Gunn, shoving her out of the bed. "Hide. Do something!"

To his surprise, Leni grabbed up her gown, slipped

51

it over her head and then climbed out the window. Then he remembered. The chair! The little scamp!

Kristina knocked on his door. Gunn sat up, felt for his shorts.

"Gunn? You awake? I can't find Leni."

He found his shorts, managed to put them on as he hopped on first one leg, then the other, toward the door. He shoved the chair aside, opened it a crack.

"Huh?" he said. "You woke me up."

She shoved the door open, brought up a candle lantern. The bed danced in the light. It was mussed up, but there was no one in it.

The backdoor slammed. Footsteps padded on the hardwood floors.

Gunn sucked in his breath.

"Kristina! So, you couldn't sleep either. I went out back for some air, to look at the stars."

Gunn let his breath out.

"I—I'm sorry I bothered you, Gunn. Go back to sleep. I guess my sister got restless."

Gunn closed the door, heaved a sigh.

Then, his knees turned to jelly and he sagged nearly to the floor.

Leni was not only an eager lover, but she was also a pretty damned good actress!

CHAPTER SIX

Gunn yelled at the top of his lungs.

Raw pain shattered his sleep, brought him rising out of bed. But he couldn't move. Someone sat on his stomach. Someone with blonde hair, ice-blue eyes and fingers that were tearing the hairs out of his chest in clumps.

"Goddamn you, bitch!"

"Gunn, you lowdown, lying bastard, you no-good sonofabitch, you took my sister and deflowered her!"

Kristina sat astraddle Gunn's middle, plucking the hairs from his chest as if she was picking blackberries. Gunn hollered again, tried to grab her wrists. He felt as if he had been tarred and feathered and someone was snatching off chunks of his flesh. His chest ran with fire.

It took him several seconds to remember where he was, what had happened. Kristina was wearing scratchy trousers, a loose-fitting blouse and she looked totally insane. Her blue eyes were wide and flashing, as threatening with pure hatred as any he'd ever seen. She tore the hairs out of his chest as fast as she could move her hands.

He brought his right fist up, and cracked her square on the jaw.

Her eyes rolled in their sockets and she went limp. He caught her in his arms as she sagged.

He squirmed out from under her. She was almost out, but her eyelids fluttered.

God, he thought, she was beautiful!

And mean, too!

"Kristina, I'm sorry. Hey, wake up. I didn't mean to crack you like that, but Jesus!"

Her eyes wobbled.

He chucked her under the chin, tapped her cheeks with mild slaps.

"Kristina?"

Her eyes opened wide. She glared at him.

"You're a no-account bastard like I thought. You deflowered Leni!"

She clenched her fists, started to strike him. He grabbed her wrists, pinned her to the bed. He had his shorts on, reeked of lovemaking. Kristina squirmed, but he applied pressure on her arms, to hold her still. He wanted her. She looked very fetching. Very fetching. Sexy. Despite his pain, his sudden anger, he wanted her. But not this way. She would have to come to him. But, as he looked into her flashing blue eyes, he was tempted. Mighty tempted. To take her right there, put the boots to her.

He released the pressure on her wrists, backed away from her.

"If you try to hit me," he said, "I'll put you away for the rest of the day."

"You would, wouldn't you? Is that what you do, Gunn? Pick on defenseless women? Like Leni? You went after her even before Pa died. Out there at the corral. She doesn't know any better. You took advantage of her."

54

"Yeah. I'm a bastard. I stalked her, raped her. I'm real mean with women, Kristina. I work 'em over like yearling calves. I hunt them down and throw 'em into the hay every chance I get. The younger the better. The innocent ones. And, it's too bad you're a spinster. I might attack you too and make your scowling face smile!"

She drew back as if he had slapped her.

A slow smile began to spread across Gunn's face.

Kristina looked at him for a long time, then a look of understanding spread across her face. She began to laugh. Quietly at first, then more loudly.

Gunn began to laugh with her.

He slid off the bed, stood up. Kristina's eyes drifted to his crotch.

"God, you are something, aren't you?"

"I'm just a man," he said, turning away. There was no reason to display it. He was hard. Kristina had gotten him hard. This was not the time nor place. His reputation with her was already bad enough. His shorts bulged with his swollen manhood. He picked up his trousers, stuck his leg in one pant. The other. He drew them up, had trouble getting them on. His hardness wouldn't go away. Not as long as she was there, staring at him. He turned, buttoning his fly.

"You don't have to do anything, do you?" she asked, a note of wonder in her voice. "You're just there, like a studhorse."

"Don't make it any worse than it is. I didn't seduce Leni, Kristina. But I'll take the blame for it."

"My God. In my father's room."

He let it go. There was no use explaining. He could only make the situation worse. He was sure that

Kristina would kick him out now. Maybe that was for the best. Two women in one house with a man was trouble. Soo Li had taught him that. The Chinese character for trouble was that sign, in fact. Soo Li. He thought about her a lot.

She was dead now, but she had loved him and given him much. Now, her wisdom came back to him, seeing Kristina there on the bed, jumping to conclusions. He had stepped into something and he wondered how fast he could ride out. If Stagg was in Oro City he could look him up on his own. Kristina could either face the truth or try as she might to fulfill her father's contracts. But, looking at her now, he realized she was no hunter. She couldn't lift a two hundred pound mule deer into a wagon, nor skin out an elk twice that size.

Gunn put on his shirt, tucked it in. His tumescence lessened. He sat, pulled on his boots. Felt his chin. He could use a shave. He stood up, retrieved his gunbelt from the bedpost.

And all the time, Kristina lay there, staring at him. Her eyes were smokey now, noncommittal. He could fathom nothing from looking into them. She was just beautiful as hell, and probably mean as a stray cat.

She sprawled out on her stomach, raised her legs in the air, crossed them. Gunn hitched on his gunbelt, regarded her with slate-grey eyes.

"I've decided to accept your offer," she said.

"What offer was that?"

"To stay on, hunt. You don't have to pay us anything. We can settle up when the contracts are filled."

"When did you make that decision? Last night?

After you found out I was a lecher?"

"Just now," she laughed. She sat up, scooted to the edge of the bed. Gunn wondered how a woman could change so quickly. One moment she was a wildcat, the next a purring kitten. Kristina had her claws sheathed now, but he could sense that she was dangerous. He kept a wary distance.

"Not going to change your mind?"

"I might."

"You better let me buy in. That way you're protected."

"All right. We'll go over the books. You make me an offer and I'll accept it. Then I'll take you to Pa's hunting grounds, get you started."

"You know where he hunted?"

"I do. He thought something like this might happen to him. I've been there many times. He never went the same way twice. There are some valleys he knows about where no other white hunter has been. Pa never hunted them out. He was very careful to map out ranges, territories."

Gunn pulled up a chair, set it backwards, sat on it, facing Kristina.

"Are you still mad at me?" he asked.

"No," she said, with a mock frown. "I know how Leni is when she drinks brandy. My fault. I should have forbidden her to touch it last night."

"So, you think the brandy made her sneak in here."

Kristina hopped off the bed, chucked Gunn under the chin, tilting his head back. She smiled into his pewter eyes.

"Of course, Gunn. You don't think it was your courtly ways, do you? Your manly body? Your . . ."

He grabbed her wrist, held it gently, but firmly.

"Enough of your teasing. I think it was Leni's hot blood, and maybe you have a little bit of it in your own veins."

Their eyes locked as if they were combatants in an arena. Kristina's blue eyes turned to frost. Gunn's were pale, noncommittal. A muscle twitched in his jaw. He squeezed her wrist a little harder.

"I'm not Leni," she said tersely. "Any man who wants me has to prove he's worthy."

"Do you hold yourself in such high esteem?"

She wrenched her wrist away from his grip, strode to the door. She stopped, turned, threw back her head. With a scornful half-smile, she replied.

"No, Gunn. It's just that I hold men, in particular men like you, in such low esteem. From now on, it's strictly business between you and me. Fair enough? And I'll keep Leni away from the brandy. You keep what you have in your godamned pants!"

Before Gunn could reply, the room jarred with the sound of the door crashing shut. He stood up, retrieved his hat from the top of the bureau. Kristina was some woman. She was hard to figure, but the best ones always were. She wasn't a shallow stream, for sure. Kristina was a deep-running river.

Leni dragged the heavy wooden case out from under her father's bed. She took a key to the lock, twisted it. The lock made a clicking sound as the key scraped metal.

"My father's hunting rifles," explained Kristina. "You can pick what you need."

Breakfast was over, the paperwork done. Gunn paid

five hundred dollars on a Denver bank draft, now owned one third of the meat contracts. The wagon was hitched, Esquire saddled.

The rifles were wrapped in oil-soaked burlap. Leni took them out of the case, one by one. Kristina unwrapped them.

"Breechloaders," she said. "This is an over-under double rifle."

Gunn picked up the rifle, turned it over in his hands. It was a Schlegelmilch, .45 caliber. The furniture was nickled brass, the lock was a Goulcher. The legend "G. Goulcher" was scrolled behind both of the hammers. The barrels' bright finish had been toned down, dulled by use. The rear sight was open, the front a brass blade, dovetailed into its slot. He hefted it, sighted it.

"Here's a box of ammunition for it," said Leni, handing him an oily cardboard box. "There's more in the tackroom."

There was a Whitney-Kennedy repeater in .56 caliber. The barrel was 47 inches long. It was a lot of gun. Leni handed him the ammunition for that one. The box seemed to weigh a couple of pounds.

"Pa loaded his own bullets," said Leni. "You'll have to do the same."

There were Winchesters, the M1866 models, but he had his M1873 in .44 caliber, a good brush gun. Finally, Leni hauled out a Sharps in its own case, complete with scope. Gunn whistled. The rifle was very new, an M1877 with a 34" barrel. It was .45 caliber, a single-shot breechloader. There had been only a few made, he knew. He had never seen one before. The rifle was over 50 inches long and the scope was powerful.

"That was Pa's favorite," said Kristina. "He just bought it this year, but he has brought down elk and antelope with it at very long ranges."

"I'll take the over and under, and this one," said Gunn. "I'll use my own Winchester for the brush, these other two for the open."

"You made a good choice," said Kristina. "Leni, put everything away. I'll get the ammunition for the Sharps. Pa just finished loading fifty rounds. The box is in the tackroom. I'll meet you outside, Gunn. You may want to say goodbye to Leni."

Gunn's face reddened slightly, but he said nothing. He helped Leni repack the case, lock it and shove it under the bed. She opened a drawer in the bureau, took out cases to fit the rifles. They were each of fringed buckskin.

"I'm sorry Kristina found out," she said. "I tried to lie, but she saw right through me."

"It doesn't matter. She's over her mad, I think."

"You don't know her like I do. You be careful out there. When she takes you to the hunting grounds she might just shoot you in the back."

Gunn felt a spider crawl across the back of his neck. His mouth tasted sour.

"You say that about your own sister?"

"You know that stableboy I told you about?"

"Yeah?"

"She heard him bragging about him and me being in the barn. The next thing I knew, the boy was laid up with a broken arm. And when that healed, he left town. So they say."

"Kristina beat him up?"

"She did. With a pistol. She made him take back all

he said and every time he started to hesitate, she twisted his broken arm. It was very embarrassing."

"What did your pa say about all this?"

"He never found out. I think people in Oro City were more afraid of Kristina than of Pa."

"I'll keep that in mind."

"Gunn? Kiss me?"

"Sure, Leni." He held her tightly in his arms, kissed her. It was a long time before she let him go.

"I still want you," she breathed.

"You want me to get a broken arm?"

She laughed, mirthlessly.

"You just be careful with Kristina. She's so changeable. One minute she looks nice and sweet and the next she's got her fists doubled up, her eyes flashing fire and she's ready to kill."

Gunn carried the rifles out to the wagon. He felt lightheaded, slightly nervous. Kristina was waiting for him. Both horses were hitched to the back of the meat wagon. Hers was a bay mare with a rifle jutting from a boot. She wore a pistol on her belt, small caliber Colt.

"You have a rifle, I see," Gunn said.

"A Winchester like yours. Hair trigger, sighted fine. It's loaded and I know how to use it."

Leni looked at them, smiled wanly at Gunn.

"Goodbye," she said. "Kristina, you hurry back home."

"I'll be back before sundown," she said. "Maybe I'll bring us some fresh game."

Kristina looked at Gunn, smiled. She walked to the front of the wagon, climbed up on the seat.

"Are you coming, Gunn?"

He hesitated. Then mentally kicked himself for a

fool. Kristina wasn't the type to shoot a man in the back. Was she? He climbed in beside her.

"You drive," she said. "The mule's name is Charlie. He knows the way."

"Haw, Charlie," said Gunn. Once the wagon was moving, he felt better. He turned to look back at Leni, but she was gone.

Kristina reached down, picked up a double-barreled shotgun. The barrels were short. She laid it across her lap, adjusted the chin-strap on her hat so that it wouldn't blow off.

"What's that for?" asked Gunn.

"Oh, I might see something I want to shoot. You just follow directions and keep that mule headed west. He's my own personal mule. Named him after the boy who gave him to me. Charlie Simms. He was right nice to give me such a good mule."

"Charlie Simms?"

"He used to mind the livery in Oroville," said Kristina. "But he left town real sudden one day."

Gunn gulped, wished she would point the shotgun the other way. Every time he looked down he could see both barrels. They looked like the vacant eyes of a snake ready to strike.

CHAPTER SEVEN

Jed Randall rode into Oro City late in the afternoon. There was a taste of snow in the air and he shrugged into his sheepskin jacket. He was a short man, about five seven in his stocking feet, with a shock of straw hair that would never lie down all at once. He was bowlegged from years spent forking a horse, chasing after cattle and trouble. His nut-brown eyes were crinkled at the corners now as he looked over the roaring city that would one day be called Leadville. Everywhere he looked there was activity. Men building, hammering, loading wagons, yelling, staggering half-drunk, peering out of hotel windows, flirting with the painted women. Music drifted out onto the street from a half dozen saloons and women sat by windows or leaned over balconies giving him free looks at their generous bosoms. Jed licked his lips, smiled back at them. Occasionally he doffed his battered hat and the women would laugh at his haystack hair. Jed rode on to Alpine House on Main Street, across from the livery stable. That was where he was to meet his friend Gunn. Today, tomorrow, whenever he showed up.

He put his horses up at the livery, the buckskin pack

horse and the claybank yellow he had ridden from Cheyenne. The bucksin he had bought in Denver after hearing the talk about Oro City. The animal was loaded with picks, shovels, pans, hammer, nails, an axe, a hatchet, spare ammunition, grub. Long before he reached Oro City, Jed Randall had the fever. Silver fever. Silver was on everyone's tongues down in Denver and all along the trail. They were talking about H.A.W. Tabor and big strikes. The Rockies were laced with not only silver, but gold, and Jed was anxious to talk Gunn into being his partner. He was sure they could become rich. Never mind that winter was coming on and the mountains would freeze over by November and never open up until May. Jed was ready.

"Any place you can keep my tools?" he asked the liveryman.

"Got a storehouse out back. Cost you extry."

"How much extry?"

"Four bits a day. Cheap. Some'll charge you five dollars a day and you'll play hob gettin' it back when you come to claim it. I got a bar lock on the storehouse an a half-breed who watches it for me. But you pay in advance and if you don't claim it pay up at the end of your time, it's mine."

"Jesus," said Randall. "I thought everybody was rich up in Oro City."

The old liveryman, with yellowed eyes, tobacco-browned fingers, a bulbous strawberry nose and wrinkled skin laughed phlegmatically. He looked at Randall's dress, his boots and saddle, the iron on his hip.

"Mister, the onliest people who makes money up

here is the skinners."

"Skinners?"

"Yessir, the skinners. And that's just about everybody in business up here. You don't watch yourself, pilgrim, they'll skin you alive!" The old man with the bronchial problem laughed until he began wheezing. "My name's Lemuel Jones, but call me Lem. I'll watch your goods for a day or a week, but ain't liable for 'em. I won't cheat you and if you ask me I'll tell you where to buy and where to eat and drink. But you want some advice, I'll tell you. They ain't a saloon in town what's honest and the whiskey'll kill you. The gals got the clap and the gents are just plain mean. Hunger and poverty does that to people. They find out you don't have a claim or work for someone already here, they'll call you out, skin you and eat you alive."

"Nice, peaceful town, huh? My name's Randall. Jed Randall. Did a man named Gunn get into town? Tall, just over six feet, grey eyes, kind of light hair that's dark sometimes, rides a big sorrel named Esquire."

"Nope. And this is the only livery in town."

Randall frowned. Some of his enthusiasm for silver mining was wearing thin. He gave Lem Jones a dollar and a half for storage, figuring he'd be three days at the most before he got a place to headquarter and paid him to grain and curry his horses at two dollars a day. He wondered how long a man's money would last in such a place.

"You stayin' at Alpine House, Randall?"

"I reckon."

"Best in town. Honest, anyways. Food's good. Single lady owns it, name of Eloise Blake. Right purty woman. Hands off, though. She's some strong on being petted out of season."

"She don't like it?"

"I wouldn't rightly know, nor nobody else. She stays to herself. Polite, mind you, but thorny if you got wanderin' hands. Just thought I'd put a bug in your ear."

"Thanks, Lem. I can't wait to meet the lady."

Jones laughed again until he went into a paroxysm of coughing. His face turned pale blue and Jed wondered if he'd make it. Jones waved him on, though, and straightened up, began dipping a battered bucket into the grain barrel.

Alpine House was the most permanent-looking structure in town. Jed looked at the ramshackle clutter of buildings with their weather-worn signs. It was like other mining towns he'd been in, except the air was thinner and there wasn't much mud. He heard the clang of metal sounding up in the hills and looked up, scanning them with interest. A few solitary flakes of snow drifted down from a leaden sky. He saw a few scaffolds clinging to cliffs, some trails and tailings, but nothing to indicate the numbers of people hurrying past him, all in a blind hurry. He crossed the street to the hotel, lugging bedrole, rifle, and saddle blanket. Men bumped into him as if he wasn't there. A small cluster of men in front of Paddy's Ale House watched him with narrowed eyes. He noticed them, ignored them. He didn't want trouble, but he saw that this would be an easy place to buy some cheap.

His boots clattered on the boardwalk, the steps to the hotel porch. Idlers talked of the weather as he passed them. A bleary-eyed man asked him for some coin. Randall dipped into his pocket, gave the man two bits.

"Don't make a habit of this," he said.

"Much obliged, stranger."

Randall opened the door of the hotel, adjusted his eyes to the dim light of the lobby. A clerk rose from a chair went behind the desk, leaving a tattered copy of The Rocky Mountain News behind.

"Room?"

"You got any without cockroaches?"

"Too high up for cockroaches," said the clerk, going along with Randall. "But we got lice, nits, bedbugs and sand fleas if you get lonesome."

"No thanks, I brought my own."

"How many nights?"

"Two, three maybe."

"Three dollars a night, twenty dollars a week. That's the cheapest."

Randall whistled.

He looked around the lobby, up the stairs.

"Funny, I don't see no shandyleer. This can't be the Brown Palace."

A woman opened a door behind the desk, came up beside the clerk. She was pretty, young, in her late twenties, early thirties. Her hair was light brown, combed back along the sides to reveal sharp, patrician features, wide blue eyes, full lips, a mole at the corner on her left cheek. She wore dangling earrings and a low-cut bodice revealing creamy mounds of breasts.

"What's the trouble here, Doug?" she said. "This man giving you trouble?"

"No, Miss Blake. He just likes to jaw, is all. Figger

he's been low on company lately and just wants to criticize the hotel."

"We have a nice clean place here," she told Randall, assessing him with practiced eyes. "Rooms are five dollars a night, take it or leave it."

"Old Doug here said three," he said, chuckling.

"Old Doug isn't the boss. I am. You can stay at some of the flophouses down the street for three dollars. We're charging five. Baths are two dollars and we have a bar here that serves Denver whiskey. If you want a chandelier in your room you're out of luck."

"Just joking, ma'am. Name's Jed Randall. I'm supposed to meet a friend of mine here."

"If he's got your taste he's probably down at the Brown Palace, Randall. Do you want a room or don't you?" Her tone was light, but Jed didn't know if she was kidding or not. His inpertinence had already cost him four dollars. If this was the best place in town he sure as hell didn't want to go down the street.

"I'll take a small room," he said. "And three's about all I could pay."

"You want a dormitory, Randall," she said, "not a private room. Five dollars. But the prices go up and down here in Oro City. It might be dearer if you wait another two minutes."

Randall put a sawbuck on the counter. Doug shoved the register at him. Jed signed with an X. Doug frowned. Eloise Blake smiled.

"The man you're supposed to meet isn't a marshal by any chance, is it?" she asked.

Jed laughed.

"No, ma'am. He's not as smart-aleck as me, either." Jed scrawled his name beside the X: Jedediah P. Randall.

"What's the P for?" asked Eloise.

Jed's face flushed crimson.

"I don't use it none," he said.

"Is it Percival?"

"No, ma'am. It's a family name. Pendragon."

"Jesus," said Doug. "They saddled you down with a four-bit word like that?"

"Yeah. My folks hated me. I was the only kid of theirs what lived."

This time, Eloise laughed.

"Enjoy your stay," she said. "Doug, give this man his change." Eloise swirled away with a rustle of skirts, went through the archway leading to the bar. Randall watched her with admiration, his eyes fixed on her bouncing bustle.

Doug shoved four dollars across the counter.

"That's some woman," Jed said quietly.

"She is that. Mighty independent too. It could be you can buy her a drink once you get cleaned up. But that's about as far as it would go."

"A shame," whispered Jed, "a damned shame."

"What's that you say?"

"Nothing. You got a key to that room? And tell me where the bath is. I can find the bar."

Fifteen minutes after Jed Randall checked into the hotel, Eloise Blake knew about his mining fever, what goods he had brought with him, what his horses looked like and everything he had told Lemuel Jones. There was one thing that puzzled her. Randall had mentioned a man named Gunn and the name rang a distant bell. Eloise Blake was a woman who wanted to know all she could about the people who drifted into

69

Oro City. She was very astute, very perceptive. She had a good memory. The name "Gunn" had triggered a memory, but she couldn't recall it, couldn't dredge it up from her mind. She sat on a stool at the bar, worrying a weak mixture of Old Crow and water.

"Slim," she said to the bartender, "the name Jed or Jedediah Randall mean anything to you?"

Slim Gailard, an extremely paunchy man who weighed close to three hundred pounds, was short as barrel keg and so bewhiskered he had hardly any face, leaned on his side of the bar, causing it to groan and creak.

"Nope," he said.

"How about the name Gunn?"

"Gunn?" he boomed. Slim had a large voice. It resounded in the bar like a thundering command. A half dozen men looked up. A couple of them reacted, narrowing their eyes to curious slits.

"Yes. Gunn. Randall says he's waiting for this man. Is he the law?"

Slim rocked back on his heels. He wiped his hammy hands on his apron. The floor boards sagged under his feet.

"Gunn," he said. "Now there's a name I haven't heard in a while. But it's a name what's been spoken a time or two at the bar and down to Denver, along Cherry Creek. Some trouble up on the Poudre. Was a man there name of Gunnison. He was some kind of hero in the War. A captain, I recollect. His wife was done in, rubbed out and he took after the bunch what did it. But he changed his name to Gunn and done a whole lot of things if you can believe the stories."

Eloise Blake was interested. She leaned over the bar, cupped her drink.

"I want to know everything there is to know about him," she said. "Anything you can think of."

"Likely it's mostly lies, Miss Blake. You know how fellers talk. This Gunn's a loner, a real hardcase. Went kind of crazy, I heard. Trouble. That's what he is, and I wouldn't let him in the hotel was I you."

"Slim, don't put me off. I want to know." Eloise's eyes flashed. She, too, had heard some stories.

"Yes'm," said Slim, and he spoke to her, telling her what he had heard. Her eyes glittered. He had seen that look before. It was the look of a woman who wanted a man. He was suprised. He realized he didn't know his boss well at all. She had always seemed so calm, so collected. But she was interested in this man Gunn, a man he knew only as a vague legend, a man spoken about in awed whispers, at campfires on the trail, in saloons, wherever men gathered and spoke about sudden death.

Jed walked into the hotel saloon reeking of lilac water and lye soap. He had pounded most of the dust out of his clothes, slicked his hair down as best as he could, cramped it under his good hat. He spotted Miss Blake at a table and angled toward her, thirsty as a longhorn ten days up to Chisholm.

"Ma'am," he said politely, as he approached her table. A man and a woman were sitting with her. Neither of them had drinks. She did, and there was a bottle on the table. "Could I buy you a hospitality drink. Smoke a peace pipe with you?"

Eloise laughed briefly.

She nodded to the couple, who rose from their chairs and went to the bar, their arms around each other's waists.

"Sit down, Jed Randall. I'll buy you a drink if you'll tell Slim over there to bring you a glass."

Jed sat down, but Slim brought a glass without any asking.

Randall felt slightly uncomfortable, as if he'd just stepped out on a stage in front of an audience. The curtain was up, the candles lit and he didn't know how he had gotten there or what was expected of him.

He poured a drink, offered the bottle to Eloise.

"No, I'm fine," she said. "I want to know what you and your friend are looking for in Oro City. Trouble?"

"Me and Gunn? No ma'am. Just rendezvousing."

"This the Gunn who ranched up on the Poudre?"

"Yes'm. You heard tell of him?"

"Just a little. There are some men in here who don't like the mention of his name. See those three at the bar? The ones with the pistols ss?"

Jed turned, looked over in the direction Miss Blake was nodding. He took a healthy swallow of the whiskey. It clawed at his throat, seared his swallower all the way down to his belly. The men looked hard. They were looking at him and he didn't like that. He had never seen them before.

"Who are they?" he asked, through tight teeth, his lips barely moving.

"They work for a man named Tolly Stagg."

Randall turned around to look at her.

"Never heard of him," he said.

"Well, those men there have heard of Gunn. I don't think they like him very much."

"I'll tell him that, when I see him."

"Uh oh," she said, looking over his shoulder. "They're coming this way. I don't know if you'll have a chance to tell him."

Randall turned around.

It was true. The three men were walking straight toward him. He didn't like the way they kept their arms hanging down, their hands hovering over their gun butts.

"Miss Blake, I come here peaceful. To buy you a drink and get me some grub, go to bed early. But it looks like I'm in for a conversation with some men I don't hardly know well enough to have coffee with. You want me to leave?"

"No. Slim there has a double-barrelled on their backs. I'm curious about what these men want to say to you. Don't worry."

"I am worried."

"I have a two-shot derringer under the table, Mister Randall. You haven't a thing to worry about."

"No? Then why do I have to go to the latrine real bad, ma'am?"

The men came on, stopped short of the table.

"What's this I hear about you being a friend of a man named Gunn?" asked a darkskinned man with a battered hat, drooping moustache. He was about thirty-five and his face looked like the business end of a single-bit axe, all pinched and mean as if he always had a case of the mads.

"Hell, I'm a friend to a lot of people," said Randall, swigging the rest of his whiskey.

Jed thought that might give him time.

It didn't.

73

One minute he was looking at the man's face and the next, another one had stepped in close and hit him with something that felt like a sledgehammer. He realized, later, that it was only a fist. An ordinary fist. But the man had brought it up from floor level and leaned into it. When it struck Jed's jaw, all the lights in the heavens and earth flashed in his brain. There was a noise like a rushing river and a deep cloud of blackness rushed toward him, smothered him. He remembered trying to smile, feeling like an idiot. He remembered reaching for his pistol and feeling a sharp pain shoot through his shoulder and arm. He remembered a big sound like a volcano erupting and someone screaming.

He remembered a dark hole opening up and swallowing him.

CHAPTER EIGHT

The sky filled with lead-grey clouds and the air turned chill. The wagon rumbled down the rutted road as Kristine slipped into a sweater. Gunn felt a gust of cold wind and knew that the weather was liable to change fast.

"Mind handing me that sheepskin back there?" he asked.

Kristine, her lips blue with cold, nodded. She climbed into the back of the wagon, found his heavy winter jacket.

"I—I didn't bring a jacket," she said.

"It's going to snow. Tonight, maybe sooner. Much farther?"

"Far enough. Pa has a place he keeps the wagon. He hunts within a half day's ride from there, brings the game back. It's high up, and he's built poles to cure the meat where the animals can't get to them."

"You better ride on back, just give me directions."

"You'd never find it," she said grimly, shivering under the sweater. Gunn tossed her his jacket.

"Put that on. I've got a Mackinaw in my bedroll. I can get it later."

A stray few flakes of snow dusted their faces.

Kristine put on the jacket. It swallowed her up and Gunn laughed.

"I don't care," she said. "It's warm."

"If it snows, you won't be able to get back."

"I'll get back. This is the best time to hunt, Pa says. Said. It's hard to think he's not out here somewhere. It's almost like I can feel him. All around me."

"I know. The spirit is a strong thing. It lingers long after a person is gone, but most people don't feel it. The Indians know this. Most of what they knew can't be seen by people."

"Do you believe in all that?"

"For a time, after Laurie died, I felt her spirit was there, on the ranch. I didn't want her there any more. So I burned it down. Burned everything up and I rode away."

"But—didn't you want to remember her? You could have stayed there, made a new life for yourself."

"No. She was murdered there, in our home. That's why her spirit stayed around so long. I could feel her there. I avenged her and that was enough. She had a better place to be."

"You're a strange man, Gunn. I haven't figured you out yet."

"Maybe we never figure out people. Maybe we're not supposed to."

The mules picked up speed going down the grade. Gunn reined them back. The road petered out after a while and Kristine had to point out the blazes on the trees. They were all different, small. Lund had done well. He had marked his trail, but it would not be easy for someone to find. Soon, he detected a pattern. The high blazes meant to go straight until the next blaze.

If the slash was low, it meant turn right 45 degrees to the next mark. If the blaze was about in the middle between high and low, it meant to turn left 45 degrees. The blazes were each about a hundred yards apart.

"I can find my way in," he said to Kristine.

"There's a camp where Pa stays. After we leave the wagon, I'll have to show it to you. He has logs up there, too, sometimes cures the game there until he begins packing it back to the wagon. All you have to do is gut out the meat and bring it up to the cabin. Leni and I do the skinning and quartering with Pa's help. We have saws there. It doesn't take long between the three of us."

Gunn said nothing. The clouds scudded in low, thickened there in the high air. The wagon path led through flat places in the woods, wound around steep dropoffs that took his breath away when he looked over the side. The temperature kept dropping and he finally stopped, dug the MacKinaw out of his bedroll. Kristine walked off by herself, returned a few moments later. More snow began to fall, but the flakes were scattered. Every so often a gust of wind would rise up an a small snow flurry would dance in the air like confetti at a parade. Gunn built a smoke, checked the mules and horses.

"You seem almost to know the way," she said, after they were moving again. I haven't given you directions in over an hour.

"Your pa's blazes have a pattern to them."

She laughed.

"He always said a good tracker could find him, but said there weren't any good trackers anymore."

"There's a few, I reckon."

"Pa built a lean-to. A log hut, with a sloping roof. If it snows too hard, there's shelter."

"What about the animals?"

"For them too. He put a roof over some logs in a little draw."

They spoke no more until the trail petered out. Gunn saw no more blazed trees. He was lost.

"Pa never went the same way twice over this last part," Kristine explained. So, even if someone followed him, they wouldn't know where he was going."

"Smart."

"It's not much farther."

The wind had risen, was knifing at them. The trees thinned and snowflakes swirled from the gusts. The snow was falling faster, the flakes larger than before. The snow was icy, wet. It would stick, Gun thought, if it lasted long enough. They crossed a wide meadow. He looked for ruts, signs that a wagon had passed through recently, but he saw no clear sign.

"Bear left," said Kristine, "toward those aspens at the edge of the meadow."

Gunn turned the team, heading toward the stand of white-barked aspens. Their leaves flickered bright yellow against the green of pine, the blue of the spruce. Some of the leaves fluttered to the ground, like coins falling through lake water in the sunlight. The sound of rustling leaves and wind filled his ears as he rounded a huge boulder. There was a wide cut through the trees behind the rock. Another large meadow came into view. A pair of deer broke from cover, their tails straight in the air, their ears perked, twitching.

"Mulies," he said. "Fat, too."

They had a good summer. They'll be moving to low ground before the week's up."

"If the snow is heavy, they'll move down tonight."

"They crossed a narrow stream, gurgling as it coursed downhill. At the far edge of the meadow, the land dropped off into a series of gullies and draws. More streams sounded on the high slopes and Gunn saw a cascading waterfall that looked as delicate as a bridal veil.

The skies turned dark and the snow fell furiously until they could see only a few feet ahead.

"You'd better go back, Kristine!" Gunn yelled above the wind. "This looks like a fullblown norther up here."

"A little farther."

He looked at her hands. They were red with cold. She put them in the pockets of his coat, tucked her mouth and chin down out of the cutting wind, into the raised up collar with its sheepskin lining.

"I can't see!" he cried. "We might get into trouble!"

The wind died and Gunn saw the steep talus slopes above the meadow. The air was very thin. They were just below timberline, above 9000 feet. He also saw the lean-to, which was much larger than he expected. When he turned around, the meadow was no longer visible. Lund had picked a good spot. A man would have to be right on it to see it. He saw the poles set crosswise over poles topped from living trees, places to hang dressed game.

"See!" Kristine exclaimed just before the wind and the snow swirled down on them from the high slopes. Their clothes and eyebrows were dusted like objects in a flour bin now. The snow was wet and clinging. Gunn hauled the wagon up, began unloading gear. Kristine helped, staggered toward the lean-to under the weight of rifles, ammunition. He unhitched the team, lead them uphill to a draw. There was a gate and he saw the shelter beyond. Lund had hay there, and the animals could be kept there behind another gate. He went back for the horses. Kristine was nowhere in sight, but he saw smoke rising from a tin chimney above the lean-to. When he returned, the wagon was empty.

He stepped inside the lean-to, ducking under the low-hanging eave. A small pot-bellied stove threw out warmth. Snow blew in behind him as he opened the elkskin drapes. There were robes of buffalo and deer all over the floor of the hut. Kristina sat propped against one wall, her boots off, wriggling her toes next to the stove.

"You found the corral all right?"

"Yes. It's blowing bad out there."

"I know. I'll wait until it's over."

Gunn looked at her hard. She looked as if she was bound to stay there for the winter.

"It could snow all night. Feels that way."

"Could be."

"We might get snowbound."

"We might."

"I'll ride back with you, most of the way. I can hunt on the way back."

"Gunn, there won't be an animal moving in this and you know it. I didn't plan it this way, but it would be dangerous to try and go back now."

She was right, of course. He just didn't like the idea

of being alone with Kristina. He felt as if she was spying on him. He would have preferred to be by himself, scout the country, see if he could find out which way the game was moving. He was disoriented. The snowfall had made him lose his bearings. The hunting was off to a bad start.

"What about Leni? She'll worry about you."

"No, she won't. She'll be all right. Pa and I were snowed in for a week up here once. Leni, too, for almost that long. She knows how it is."

The wind whistled through a crack somewhere. But it was warm in the lean-to. Gunn saw the dry logs stacked in a far corner. A spider crawled along the bark, drawn from its hiding place by the heat. Gunn sat down, sprawled out, leaned against his saddle. He took off his hat, wiped the sweat band dry, put it back on. His eyes flickered as he gazed around the lean-to. There was a water bucket, a cast-iron pitcher, some pots and pans hanging from nails. An old coat made of buffalo hide, a battered hat. There were pallets for sleeping. A man could survive pretty well. The roof had a steep slope so the snow wouldn't cave it in. The heat would melt most of it as it fell.

"Gunn?"

"Yeah."

"Are you sorry I'm here?"

"No, sorry isn't the word."

"But you'd rather I wasn't."

"That's closer to it."

"Why?"

"I worry about people. I came here to hunt. I work better alone."

She was quiet for a while, studying him. He rolled a

smoke, lit it. The wind keened against the lean-to now and snow blew in through the hide drapes that served as a door. The flakes melted as soon as they hit. Gunn lit his quirly, drew the smoke deeply into his lungs. He could feel the tension now. Kristine seemed to be spoiling for a fight. He sensed that she was possessive of this place, resented his being there. She was probably thinking about her father and of the times they had enjoyed up here in the high lonesome where solitude reigned like a quiet queen.

Kristine got up, went outside. She was back in a moment, red-faced, dusted with snow. Her hands were wet, rosy from the cold. A mass of flakes followed her insde. The wind whined through the trees.

Gunn finished his cigarette, threw another log on the fire. The door to the stove clanged loudly as he slammed it shut. Kristine jumped at the sound, then dipped her lashes, looked down at her cold hands. Her socks were damp and she took them off, laid them out to dry near the stove. Gunn looked at her feet. They were so naked, he felt embarrassed.

"Is there something wrong?" she asked. "I didn't make the weather."

It was Gunn's turn to jump. Her question surprised him. And he had not heard her speak for almost a half an hour.

"No."

"I get the feeling you hate me."

"No."

"You wish Leni was here. Maybe I should have sent her in my place."

Gunn's jaw twitched as his skin tautened with a

brief flare of anger.

"Dammit, Kristine, quit burring me. You got something in your craw, get it out. It's a damn small place here. I know you can't go back. We got us a real bad storm. Try to make the best of it."

"You mean leave you alone. Let you ignore me. I feel like I'm just another buffalo rub here, a lump, something for you to wipe your feet on."

Gunn's eyes rolled in their sockets. There was no understanding women. They talked all around a thing and it was hard getting the truth out of them. Not that he wanted the truth. He just wanted to be left alone.

"I'll check the horses and mules, see if they got enough hay." He stood up, grabbed his Winchester, started to leave.

Kristine stood, ran over to him.

"You don't have to go out there! You're just being cruel."

"Kristine, dammit, I don't know what you're talking about!"

Her hands lashed out, grabbed him by the arms. She spun him around to face her.

"Kiss me!" she commanded. "Hold me. Do anything you want! But don't ignore me. I can't take that, not after what you and Leni did last night!"

He looked into her flashing eyes, felt the pain, the torture she was feeling. It made things more easy to understand, but not simpler. Kristine had a case of jealousy. A bad case.

He grabbed her roughly, let his rifle slip from his fingers. He drew her to him, kissed her hard on the mouth. He crushed her lips brutally, bent her head back until he thought her neck would snap. If that's what she wanted, he'd give it to her good, then be done with it. He tried to break the kiss, figuring he had hurt her enough. But she clung to him and her lips moved invitingly. Her body thrust against his and he felt her loins grinding into his own. He felt her heat and he smelled the fragrance in her hair. Her breasts burned against his chest. He felt her heat and her hunger.

Was it possible that Kristine was more of a woman than Leni? She was hungrier, deeper, more savage. Her lips mashed his own and he felt the salty taste of blood. She pulled him down and her legs crumpled. He fell on top of her and still she did not break the kiss. She drew an arm around his neck and pulled him tightly against her.

And he wanted her then, more than he had ever wanted another woman.

CHAPTER NINE

Eloise Blake brought the derringer up out of her lap.

Slim Gailard slid the double-barreled shotgun across the top of the bar. He hammered back. Two loud clicks sounded in the silence.

"Packer, you step away from that man or I'll blow a hole in your heart," said Eloise calmly. "You had no right to hit him. He was my guest."

Reece Packer was the man who had slugged Jed Randall. He was a leanly muscular man with well-developed shoulders, oversized fists. His face wore a permanent scowl watched over by close-set, deepsunk eyes of glittery hazel. He was bald under his hat, prematurely, because he was only thirty-two years old. The other two with him were Morton Brown and Alf Suggs. At the moment they worked for Tolly Stagg, but they had worked for a number of men over the years and most of what they did was illegal.

"This man's a pard of Gunn's and that makes him an enemy," said Packer.

"What have you got against Gunn?" asked Eloise.

"Private business."

"Gunn rubbed out a kid used to ride with us, Randy

85

Cocker. His pa, too. And a bunch we knew some years back got 'dobe walled by this same jasper." Alf Suggs got a dirty look from Packer for his outburst, but Brownie grinned and licked his livery lips. He was a sickly pale man with a moon face and reddish lips that made him look effeminate. But he was a hardcase and his hand was never very far from his pistol butt. Suggs was a lean gangly man with a sharply pointed Adam's apple that looked as if it would tear through his skin at any moment. He had a three-day beard on his face that grew in unevenly.

"Coker. The man who killed Gunn's woman," said Slim at the bar. "He was a no account."

"It was never proved," said Packer. "But you asked me a question, Miss Blake and I'll tell you why I laid this Randall low. We was up in Cheyenne a-workin' and this Gunn was hired by the Cattleman's Association. He worked outside the law, killed a lot of good men. Bushwacked them. Backshot them. And then he left his brand on them. They ain't the last been heard of that business. They's some talk in Cheyenne about bringing Gunn back up and putting his neck in a rope. I figger wherever Gunn is, there's going to be some prime dirty work. You take up with saddle tramps like this Randall and Gunn will be here for sure. He don't fight fair."

"He just works for the man who pays the most for his gun," said Suggs. "He's a killer."

Eloise sucked in a breath.

"Anybody else here feel the same?" she asked aloud. Men at the bar nodded, grumbled, turned away.

"Slim?"

"I've heard both sides. That Cheyenne business was

bloody all right. But the rustling stopped. I heard Gunn did it for a friend."

"He's a hired gunny," said Packer. "He comes to town, you got yourself trouble, Miss Blake. Now if you'll just let us drag that waddie out of here, we'll get rid of some of it before it happens."

Eloise wasn't sure. She didn't want trouble, but Randall had not seemed so bad. Certainly he was polite and didn't appear to be looking for trouble. It could be that Packer and his cronies were jumping to conclusions. They had been edgy lately. Tolly was in and out, up to something. He wanted the meat contract, of course, but Lund wouldn't sell out. He had managed to acquire some silver claims, but these men were not miners. Their hands had no callouses on them. Gunn was the question mark. Was he a hired killer? Had something happened up there on the Poudre to make him go bad? Slim's assessment was not clear on that. Packer had his side of it.

The Blake family had settled Colorado in the late fifties. Eloise's father, Martin, had been a newspaperman, then a miner, and finally earned enough to build a nice home on a hill above Cherry Creek, away from the city of Denver. His wife, Amelia, was devoted to him and they now had comfortable lives. The Blakes were well known and Martin had been involved in the political aspects of statehood since the beginning. Eloise had struck out on her own with money her father had given her and had realized that the real money to be made in mining, the steady money, was from the throngs of dreamers who went to the boom towns, who grew crazy with the fever. She could spot them now. Her philosophy had paid off because she didn't gouge the customer; she provided good bed and board and honest drinks. If her gamble in Oro City paid off, she planned to open a number of hotels, calling them all Blake House, all through the Rockies. Oro City, she felt, was destined to be a good city, one that would last beyond the boom. Randall was one of those men who had that look about him. She was sure he would catch the fever if he hadn't already. The tools he had brought with him told her that, but there was something else. A look in his eyes, a restlessness. He was, on appearance, one of those who might stick, who might strike it rich and stay on to help build a permanent city in the mountains.

"Packer, no deal," she said, making up her mind. "Randall's a guest here and so far he has comported himself well. You are the one who seems bent on causing trouble. I'll ask you once, and once only, to leave my establishment for the evening. You, Brownie and Suggs."

Packer scowled.

"We paid for a bottle," he said.

"Take it with you. Just get out. Now!"

She cocked the derringer for emphasis. The three men backed off, still facing her.

"We'll take care of Randall another time," said Brownie.

"Yeah," agreed Suggs.

"Not in here, you won't."

The tension hardened in the room. The three men took their bottle, left noisily. She heard them clump down the street toward Paddy's. They were in an ugly mood. She eased the hammer back down on the derringer, breathed a sigh of relief.

"Slim," she said. "Help me get this man on his feet. He needs a meal and a good night's sleep."

Kristina clawed at Gunn's clothes. A savage light flickered in her eyes. She panted with eagerness. Gunn worked the buttons free of their holes on her shirt, spread the blouse wide to reveal her heaving breasts. She ran her fingers through the hairs on his chest, ran her tongue over wet lips.

"I want you, Gunn," she husked. "I want to just crawl inside you." Her fingernails scraped his flesh like talons. Her teeth grated together.

He stripped her naked, shucked his own clothes.

They embraced frantically. Kristina squirmed against him as if trying to get inside his skin. She was voluptuous, her skin soft. He fondled her breasts, tweaked her nipples until they hardened into rubbery kernels.

A faint cherry light leaked from the potbellied stove, splashed their naked bodies with gold. The wood crackled in the silence hemmed by the razoring wind. The faint light of afternoon lit the lovers, too, when the wind opened the hide-draped doorway and blew in ragged flakes of snow.

Gunn put his mouth on one of her breasts, drew the nipple between his lips. She arched her back, thrust her loins into his. She wallowed beneath him like a woman being tortured, and he felt her hand find his stalk, grasp it with a tender squeeze. He suckled her breasts, and let his hand roam her valleys and the concave places of heat, find the nest between her legs. She groaned with pleasure, sucked at the flesh of his arms and chest with a vampire's urgency. Her hand pulled

89

on his manhood, made it swell and throb until it was a pulsing beast in her palm.

Gunn slid down her chest, over her belly, with his mouth. She released her handhold on his cock and grasped his hair as he nuzzled the nest between her legs. He buried his nose in her loins, then parted her labials with his tongue. Kristina cried out and tugged at his hair. He lanced her delicate flesh again and again with his stabbing tongue. Tasted her dark honey, smelled her heady musk. Felt her squirm and clamp his head with rhythmic scissoring thighs.

"Gunn, don't! Stop! I—I can't stand it!"

He looked up, over the gentle rise of her tummy.

"You don't like it?"

"Oh no! I love it! I just—just can't stand it," she said breathlessly. "It's something I—I never even thought of. I—I'm ashamed. Not in the way you think, but just ashamed of how dumb I've been. A man, doing this to me. I—I just never dreamed anything could be so natural, so beautiful, so—exciting."

He slid back up her body, faced her, close.

"You taste good, Kristina."

She made a mock show of hiding her face. Then, she peeked through her hands at him. Smiled. He smiled back.

"Do you know what you do to me? To a woman. To kiss a woman there is the most beautiful thing that could happen to her."

"I don't know," he said. "A woman's body has so many good places to kiss, it's not hard at all to find one to touch or feel. I think any man who doesn't know what makes a woman feel good, doesn't feel too good himself."

She stared at him for a long time, as if awestruck.

"I—I never heard anything so wise," she said. "Not in all my borned days. Gunn. Where did you come from? Who are you?"

"We lived in Arkansas. I'm just an ordinary man."

"No," she breathed, letting her head fall on one folded arm, looking up at him with shining eyes, "you are not ordinary. Not you, Gunn. Your Laurie must have been very special. Your eyes. I've never seen any so pale. And when you touch me, with a finger, your hand, your lips, I feel as if lightning is striking me, as if there is fire at the end of your fingertips."

He didn't say anything. He looked at her, and she was very beautiful, lying there with her clothes all off, a thin sheen of sweat on her skin. Her breasts so full and the nipples taut as unripened plums, the aureoles dark and bumpy, perfectly circular. He wanted her and his cock throbbed and bobbed up and down like a spear in the hands of a nervous man. She talked too much and the talk make him feel like a piece of pottery on a drummer's blanket. He had tasted her body because it pleased him, because he lusted for her. There was no mystery to that. He was not special. He felt her heat and it was a thing he could understand. Kristina was a woman a man wanted to sex in every way possible. She flowed like great majestic clouds, like mountains, like sensuous deep rivers. She was a pillow, a hearth, a wanton in a great wide bed that was silk-sheeted and soft.

"I've embarrassed you, haven't I? I'm sorry. I didn't mean to. Gunn. Listen to me. I've been with men before. Oh, Leni doesn't know that. And neither did Pa. I guess that's why I was so mean to her. I didn't want

91

her to sneak it like I did. I wanted her to be a virgin, to meet a good man, marry, raise a nice family. I wanted for her what I wanted for myself. But I was weak. Or hotblooded, whatever you want to call it . . ."

"Kristina," he said, "you don't have to tell me all this. You don't have to talk about . . ."

"Hush, now, I have to say this now. I've kept it inside me so long I'm about to burst. You are different. I can see that now. You listen. You care. So, let me say my say because it's important right now."

"Yes."

"The men—they were all shadows. Men I wanted and desired. Who would give me what I wanted. I thought. They gave me something, I suppose. Five minutes, a thrill lasting a second or two. Not really what I wanted, but I didn't know that until a few minutes ago. I took them anywhere I could. In a room, a barn, a stable, on the prairie. Stolen moments . . . cheap satisfactions of the flesh . . ."

"Don't, Kristina," he said. "You don't have to shame yourself like this."

He dabbed at the tears streaking down her cheeks.

"Gunn, oh Gunn. Thank you for making me see. Now, I want to return the favor. No, that's not the right word. I want to love you as you have loved me. In that way. That special way. No man ever kissed me there before. No man ever cared about me. I was—was becoming hateful of men. All men. I hated you. I hated what you—what I thought you did to my sister. But I saw her this morning. She was happy. She was glowing. I know that it must have been—beautiful. As this is beautiful to me."

She rose up, then, and twisted her body until she had reversed her position. Gunn watched her slide toward him, felt her hand touch his manhood. He lay back, let her have her free rein. Her back was lovely, smooth, the cords of her spine visible under her skin. He touched it, stroked it with a single finger, traced a path to the crease of her buttocks.

Kristina squeezed his cock, bent her head. She took his penis in her mouth, gingerly. He felt her hesitation, knew that she had never done this before. An electric charge shot up through his loins. Her lips nibbled on the sensitive, velvety crown of his organ. A delicious agony coursed through his stalk. He wanted to plunge it into her mouth, bury it in the moist heat, sink it there to stay until his juices bubbled and exploded.

"Oh," she moaned, "it tastes so nice. It's so hard, so big."

"Kristina," he said. "You don't have to do this."

"I want to, Gunn. I want to!"

She swallowed him then and he felt the surge of seed in his sac. Her mouth enveloped him and her lips squeezed tight below the crown of his cock. He sank deep and felt her suction draw him still deeper. The head of his manhood touched her throat and slid along its lining. He grasped her hair, hung on like a man at the edge of a terrible cliff.

She suckled him, learning as she went. Her head bobbed up and down, her mouth squished with the pumping of him as she drew his manhood past her lips. He touched her breasts and she twitched as if spasming with orgasm. She moaned and made strange sounds. And she would not turn loose of him until he pulled her head back and forced her onto her back. Her mouth was wet, her lips beestung, raw, livid with color.

"Enough, Kristina," he growled. "I want inside you. I want to give you what I have face to face."

"Oh, god yes," she sighed. "I—I just loved it so much. I could feel your blood pulsing, I could taste you and I gushed inside like I never did before."

"You came?"

"A hundred times."

He marveled at her. He kissed her delicately on the lips and embraced her. He dipped into her, slid his manhood past the puffed lips of her sex and into the oven of her womanhood. She buckled and cried out. She thrashed, climaxed as he speared deeply into her willing burrow.

"Gunn," she breathed, "this is what I was looking for. All the time. Oh, yes. This. Just this and no more. I have given my body before, but . . ."

"You don't need to say anything," he panted, rising and falling above her. "You don't have to say a damned thing."

"No. I don't, do I? But I begged before. I begged those men. And they treated me like the beggar I was."

"You don't have to beg, Kristina."

She turned her head, and he saw fresh tears slide down her cheek. He kissed them, tasted the saltiness, the faint warmth. He drove deep and held onto her tightly as she bucked against him with an involuntary convulsion. She was sweet and warm in his arms, and she had no reason to cry. Not for this nor for her past. For Kristina, there was no past. Nor for either of them at that crystalline moment in time.

He loved her for a long while and the snow fell thickly on the land and it became night.

But the lovers inside the lean-to had no knowledge of time or the weather and they did not hear the sniffing wolves that came close during the night above the sound of the crackling flames in the potbellied stove.

CHAPTER TEN

Tolly Stagg scratched the stubble on his chin, unslung the binoculars from around his neck. He looped the strap over the saddle horn, drew a cigar out of his vest and bit off the end savagely. His horse snorted, started to back away from the precipice. Tolly rammed big-roweled spurs into the big bay's flanks and brought him back to the edge. He lit the cigar with stubby hands cupping the flame from the falling snow. He was a big man with a wide chest, barrel belly and waist. His nose had been broken and flattened until it was a distorted mushroom above a bushy moustache. His close-set blue eyes were slightly crossed, which gave him an odd, demented look. His lips were thick, flattened as his nose, spreading up into his moustache, dripping toward his chin. His hair on head and face and crotch was rust-red. His chest was hairless under the mackinaw shirt and fur-lined jacket he wore.

"What you make of it, Carp?"

Smoke from the cabin below drifted through the falling snowflakes until it disappeared in the grey drip of clouds. They had watched the cabin for a long time, wondering who was in there. The wagon had pulled out early in the day, but neither person was Grandy Lund. So, either Lund was still inside, laid up, or he had help. One of the horses he had recognized, but not the other. And the one person on the seat of the wagon could have been either a man or a woman, it had been hard to tell. No one had come out of the cabin, but now there was smoke rising from the chimney. Someone was there, but who?

"Maybe Lund got hurt. I don't see no fresh game and that wagon didn't go to town." Seth Carpenter was a fair tracker, a passable shot. The main thing was that he was dumb and loyal, two attributes that Stagg liked in a man. He didn't ask questions or argue. He did what he was told and he did it fairly well as long as someone was along to remind him of what he was supposed to do.

"You tracked it how far again?"

"Way off the regular road to Oro City, Tolly. I didn't get too close like you said so they wouldn't see me. I think one of em's that older girl, Katrina."

"Kristina, Carp. Dammit. She goin' to meet Grandy or takin' his fuckin' place?"

"Hell, I don't know," Carp drawled. He was lean, blonde-haired, with big brown eyes, freckles on his colorless face, thin lips, a razor straight nose and snaggle-toothed. Staggs had hired him in Cheyenne after seeing Carp beat a man to death without changing the expression on his face. He hadn't smiled or frowned. He had just methodically killed a man with his bare hands. A bigger man than he, in size. But Carp did not fight fair. He had upended the man, bit his ear off, smashed him in the balls, sat on his chest until the man was completely helpless, and then hammered his face to a bloody pulp with the butt of his pistol.

"All right. This goddamned snow's sticking and we got to do something. I wanted to take Lund out today, but the bastard's either spotted us and lyin' low or else out there. Can't figger him hunting without the wagon, though. He's behind and he'll lose his contract he don't bring in some meat pronto."

"He's got a week, I reckon."

"Dammit, I know that. That's why I wanted to kill him when he lit out. We missed him somewhere yesterday. That wagon bein' in the yard threw me. I can't figger it out."

Carp said nothing. It was true. They had tracked Lund yesterday morning, then lost him. But he hadn't gone far. They circled, doubled back and got lost. Darkness had caught up to them and they'd had to quit. Morning had helped them get their bearings, but Tolly had been griping that they had missed something. Something had happened that they had ought to have known about and now the mystery was deeper than before. Tolly blamed him, he knew, but he got confused with all that circling and back-tracking. Once he had seen blood and the tracks of another horse, but he had not mentioned this to Stagg. They would have lost more time wandering around. Stagg was a very impatient man. Even now, Carp knew, he was anxious to get back to Oro City. They had drunk up the last of the whiskey, slept out in the cold and now he couldn't figure out what had happened to Grandy Lund. Maybe Lund had fooled them. Maybe he was hunting, shooting game and that Katrinka or Katerina, whatever her name was had hired another hand to help him. But he didn't want to talk about that with Tolly. He was mad enough already.

"We got to go down there, find out," said Tolly, drawing on his cigar until the end glowed like an angry eye.

"He might be waitin' for us, Tolly."

"In a little while the snow will be so thick he won't be able to see twenty yards. 'Sides, they's a blind side we can sneak up on if'n we're careful. Use the tackroom for cover and then come up to the cabin on the corner. We won't make a sound on the fresh snow."

"I'm gettin' cold and hungry, Tolly."

Stagg didn't hear Carpenter. He was already going over it all in his mind, planning how he would ride back of the ridge and come up on the other side of the cabin where corral, barn and tackroom were located. He chewed on the end of his cigar until it was a soggy mass, until it would no longer draw. Then he backed the bay gelding up, swung him into the trees, ducking under a branch of a juniper.

"Where we goin' Tolly?"

"Just follow me, Carp. We're going to find out a thing or two."

"I'm hungry," said Carp, his voice so low it was smothered by the snow and blown back into his mouth by the gusting wind.

Leni watched the snow start to fall, then began to close the shutters. She knew she ought to go outside and close the outside shutters, but it did not look as though it would be much of a storm. Then, the wind began to blow and she put cloth in the cracks in the front room shutters. The room had already turned cold, and she built a fire in the fireplace. Luckily, there was plenty of wood inside. She would have to go outside later, to feed the horse in the corral, but that could be done before sundown.

As she was chinking up the windows at the back of the cabin she saw movement on the ridge to the east. At first she thought it was a deer, or an elk. But then she saw something shiny. Her heart started to pound. A man was watching the cabin through binoculars. She huddled there, peering through the crack in the shutter, until she saw another man. Her blood froze.

As she watched, the men backed away from the precipice and disappeared.

Leni quickly checked the front and back doors. Made sure they were latched securely. She knelt down, dragged out the crate containing her father's rifles, took two of them out, loaded them. She put one at the front door, one at the back. She took a gunbelt, holster and pistol from a drawer in the bedroom, made sure it was loaded. It was a Colt .38 and she knew how to use it. She strapped it on, added more wood to the fire and took a position at the back door. She stood on a chair to see through a crack above the jamb. The snow fell faster now, the flakes much bigger. She scanned the ridge back of the house. The wind blew against the cabin, whistling, whining, adding to her nervousness. She saw nothing, but she knew two men were out there. She could sense them.

The snow fell thick, blotting out the ridge.

Leni climbed down from the chair, leaned against the door.

Her heart fluttered with fear. Every sound made her jump.

"Stop it," she told herself. "Kristina will be back any minute. She'll know what to do."

The minutes dragged by. They seemed like hours.

Tolly stopped his horse in a stand of aspen.

Carp rode up alongside him.

"Look there," said Stagg, pointing.

"Fresh grave."

"Human, too. Fresh columbines on it. Let's take a look-see."

The men climbed down, tied up their horses, walked to the grave. Tolly scraped off the snow, picked up a handful of dirt. The dirt was soft, wet, crumbly.

"Dug this morning," he said.

"Who'd they bury, you reckon?" Carp felt uneasy. He didn't like graves. He didn't like being around dead people.

"Figger it out, Carp. The older daughter goes off with a stranger. No sign of Lund. Don't know. Could be the young gal. Or, it could be Lund himself."

"So, that's why we ain't cut his trail."

"Could be. Let's get down there, see what we see."

"What if Lund's there?"

"We'll find out soon enough. He says anything, we tell him it's a social call . . ."

"Somethin' spooky about all this, Tolly."

"You mind your senses, Carp. Way I figger it, Lund died and the gals hired a man to help 'em fill out the old man's contract. That means Leni's probably in that cabin. All by her lonesome."

Carp grinned idiotically. Tolly winked at him.

"Might have some fun fer ourselves," said Stagg.

Carp was no longer hungry or uneasy. He glanced at the cabin, a dark shape at the bottom of the hill. The snow was so thick he could no longer see the smoke. But he imagined young Leni Lund inside, all alone, helpless. He licked his lips, tasted fresh snow-flakes.

The two men followed Tolly's original plan. They tied their horses securely away from the grave, back in the scrub pines. Then, using the barn as cover, they crept down the hill. They carried only six guns, left a dirt-streaked trail through the fresh snow. At the barn, they waited.

"Quiet as a mouse," said Tolly.

"Reckon she knows we're out here?"

"Could be Lund inside, but I doubt it."

"That warn't no kid's grave up there," said Carp.

"You cover. I'll get over the corner of the house. When I signal, you come on."

Carp nodded, drew his pistol. Tolly drew in a deep breath, held it, then dashed toward the corner of the cabin. Carp watched him, ready to cock and fire if there was any need. Tolly made it all right, rested against the logs. Then he motioned for Carp to follow him.

"What now?" asked Carp after he had made it over from the barn.

"You take the front, I'll go in the back."

Carp frowned.

"What's the matter, Carp? You got a burr under your saddle?"

"What if Lund's in there? Waitin' at the front?"

"Oh, for Christ's sake! You want the back? Take the

102

back. Hell, they ain't no one in there but that young gal and she's probably knittin' by the fire."

Carp's eyes sparkled.

"I'll take the back," he said. "What do I do? Knock?"

"Just break in, Carp. Hell, you think she's gonna open the back door for you?"

"Don't, Tolly. You know I don't like to be ragged."

"All right. Give me time to get around front. You count to twenty after I turn the corner of the cabin. Then you run up there and bust in. Can you do that?"

"I can count to a hunnert," said Carp proudly.

Tolly nodded, ran toward the front of the cabin. He stopped there, pointed a finger at Carp. Carp began counting half out loud. He got to ten and got mixed up, so he ran up the steps, hit the back door with his shoulder. It creaked and the wood groaned, but the door didn't open. He stepped back, lifted his leg and kicked hard at the place where he thought it would be latched.

The door gave and he kicked it again.

A woman screamed.

Leni heard something hit the back door.

Her blood froze. Her heart seemed to leap into her throat, stick there like a gob of mud.

Again, something crashed against the door. She saw the latch quiver. She grabbed the rifle away from the door, backed up several feet, raised the barrel to aim chest-high. Frantically, she cocked the Baker over-and-under. The top barrel was loaded with a .45 caliber round, the bottom with a .12 gauge shotshell. The shotshell had #22 shot in it. She was glad her

103

father had two such weapons.

There was a silence. She heard bootheels pounding on the porch. Her mouth dried to a sandy crispness. Her palms eked sweat until they were slick with the oils of fear.

She heard the racing footsteps again. The door crashed open. A man stood there, pistol in hand.

"Get out!" she screamed.

The man raised his pistol. Snow swirled around him and the wind blew into her face.

"Put it down, little girl," he said.

Leni recognized him then, even with the snow flocked on his hat and his clothes. A man she had seen in town, one of Stagg's bunch. He stood there, staring at her in a way she didn't like, a way that made her feel unclean, naked. His eyes flickered with an unwholsome light. He opened his mouth and she saw spittle at the corners. She shuddered inwardly, felt a twinge of fear that made her heart sink like a stone.

A crashing noise sounded at the front of the house. She started to turn, then thought better of it after she saw the man start towards her. The front door was barred and she hoped it would hold. But, suddenly, she knew she had to fight for her life. No one would help her. There were at least two men trying to break in, violate her privacy. She saw red. The red of fire and the red of sun and the red of hard angry blood. Her house, her home, was being invaded by men she hated. Men who took certain things for granted. Kristina's words came back to memory. Men wanted only one thing from a woman and they were dangerous if you did not lead them or turn them away nicely. If you feared them, they would take you, brutally, forcefully, cruelly.

"What do you want?" she asked, her voice full of trembles and quivers.

"Just you, little gal," said Carp, drooling. "Won't be bad for you."

"You—you just go away!"

Carp's face hardened to a mask. He brought up his pistol higher.

The front door rattled and boomed with the force of someone trying to break in to the cabin.

The red in Leni's eyes blurred all thought.

Angered, full of fear, she put her finger on the trigger that would fire the .45 barrel.

Carp saw her move, started toward her.

The moment he did move, he knew it was all wrong. He wanted to back up, start all over again. He had been looking at her breasts, her pretty face, her hair, her eyes. And now he saw her face change. He saw her finger inside the trigger guard.

Leni saw him lunge toward her.

She squeezed the trigger instinctively. Smoke and flame belched from the top barrel of the Baker. Hot powder stung her face, peppered her eyes.

The .45 lead ball struck Carp in the middle of his chest, shattering his breastbone, smashing through bone and vein and vessel. The soft lead splintered, splaying through soft lung and heart muscle. A black hole opened up in his chest and a big red hole the size of a man's fist opened up in his back. A look of stark surprise lit his face. His finger touched his trigger, reflexively, and his pistol fired, filling the air with the sharp smell of black powder. The ball hummed over Leni's head, thunked into a ceiling rafter.

Carp opened his mouth to say something, but a well

of blood filled his mouth and he choked. His legs crumpled and he fell to the floor, mortally wounded.

Leni stared at him in horror.

She had never shot a man before. Never killed a man.

Carp rolled over on his back. The floor pooled with blood. He looked up at her with glazed eyes. His hand relaxed, releasing his pistol. He twitched, blood pouring from his mouth and then rolled half-over. He gave a gasp and blood gushed from his mouth in cloudy bubbles.

"No!" gasped Leni.

She heard another sound from the front of the house and turned, her finger still in the trigger guard. She fired down the hall, without thinking.

The front door crashed.

Frantic, Leni ran down the hall. She threw the rifles to the floor, almost tripped on it. She drew her pistol.

The front door sagged. A man pushed through, pistol in hand.

Leni cocked her .38, raised it with both hands. Fear drove her. Fear and loathing of what she had done. She had killed a man. Nothing could erase that. And now, she might have to kill another. Survival. That was the urgency of the moment. She had to survive!

Tolly Stagg stepped through the broken door.

Leni pointed her pistol at him.

"I—I'll shoot you," she said.

Stagg hesitated.

"Hold on," he said, soothingly. "I mean you no harm."

"You do."

"Your pa dead? We came to pay our respects."

For a moment she thought she must be mad. Maybe she had made a mistake. Maybe the men had come because her pa had died. What if she had killed a man for no reason? But no! He had come after her. And she had seen the look in his eyes. But what was Stagg saying?

"You put down your gun, Tolly Stagg!"

"Fiery, ain't ye?"

"Put it down."

Tolly set his pistol gently on the floor. He moved very slow, very careful.

"Sorry about your pa," he said.

"How'd you know he was dead?"

"Saw his grave up there."

"Yes. Now you go."

"Who killed him? Or did he die natural?"

"A man named Gunn . . . but he didn't mean to . . . I mean . . . why you askin' all these questions?"

"I, uh, just wanted to help if I could. I liked your pa. I . . ."

Suddenly, she realized, he was lying. Tolly had started toward her. She pushed her pistol toward him, cocked it.

"Get out of here, Tolly Staggs, and take that dead man with you. If you don't, I'll shoot you dead, I swear!"

"I will, I will, but back off, will you?"

"Just go on through to the kitchen and go out the back door. Kristina will be back in a while and she wouldn't let you get off so easy."

"No, I spect not. Be careful with that, Leni. I'll get my man and be on my way."

Leni felt confident, then. She felt the power of the

107

pistol in her hand. She stepped aside, followed Stagg to the kitchen. She watched him heft the dead man onto his shoulder and walk out through the back door.

He stopped at the bottom of the steps and looked back up at her.

"Can I have my pistol back?"

"I'll leave it in town at the Alpine House next time I'm in."

"You make it hard on a man, girl."

"Get goin', Tolly, before I shoot you too. You're no good. Me and my sister will fight you."

"Your sister ain't here. She got a new man? This Gunn?"

Leni saw red again.

She squeezed the trigger, fired a shot over Stagg's head. He moved, then, lumbering toward the snowy slope with a dead man on his shoulders. The dark started to move in and the snow blotted him out as he climbed up the hill. Leni went back inside, shoved the door shut. It sagged there. She knew how to fix it. The kitchen smelled of black powder and death. There was blood on the floor.

She looked at the pistol in her hand. Blueblack, ugly. Yet, beautiful.

"Kristina," she said to herself, "come back!"

Later, when she had nailed up the doors, put fresh wood on the fire, she sat in her father's chair, the pistol in her lap.

She thought of Gunn and Kristina. She wondered where they were. She wondered why she was alone.

And the wind howled and snow blew against the cabin until she closed her eyes and fell asleep as the fire crackled and sparked in the October hearth.

CHAPTER ELEVEN

Kristina made a shrine out of his manhood. She stroked him hard until his shaft towered from the dark thatch between his legs. She lay with her head close to its base, staring at it with shining eyes. Firelight flickered over the stalk, gliding it with a yellow and gold patina. She moved in on it, began flicking her tongue over the root rising out of the flesh of his thighs. Her tongue traveled up its length, to the crown. She drew herself closer, and hovered him, her finger curling around the base as she bent to suckle him. She pulled the head into her steaming mouth and felt a twinge of delight. Her lips quivered, her loins twitched with a quick electric shock.

"Ummm," she moaned, drawing his cock in and out of her mouth.

Gunn awoke with a start.

A damp warmth flooded him and he saw her hair shimmering in the stove light, a portion of her face, her lips swollen with him, distended.

It took him several seconds to get his bearings. He had been deep in sleep, layered over with fatigue and the quiet now and he reached out for her, his hand touching her tawn back. Her body was all curves, gracefully arranged, the hips round and comely, the legs slightly apart, slender, a lone breast hanging like ripened fruit from her breast, the other invisible to him.

"Kristina," he husked.

"Oh, Gunn," she moaned, "I wanted you again. I couldn't help myself." She looked up at him with wet lips. "I put some wood on the fire and started playing with you. I never saw anything get so hard so fast. It just grew and grew."

"It's late?"

"Early. Almost dawn. It stopped snowing and I have to get back."

He saw cracks of light beginning to appear in the lean-to's ceiling, faint slivers, dull and hazy.

"I did sleep, then," he teased.

"Do you think I'm terrible?"

"No. Just excited."

"I—I couldn't sleep much. I wanted you all night."

"And now?"

"Yes, Gunn. Don't make me beg."

"You don't have to beg, Kristina. Ever."

He grabbed her shoulders, lay her down on her back. He went to her, kissed her mouth until her body bowed and thrust at him. He entered her quickly. She gasped and her eyes went wide with wonder. He drove deep and fast, slowing when Kristina bucked with orgasm, lingering at the high peaks and the valleys of her excitement. Loin smacked against loin, the sound like a crackling fire as they loved each other desperately.

When it was over, he held her until the morning light filled the lean-to, and she could no longer stay.

She got up slowly, holding on to him as long as she could, letting her fingers play over his skin. He watched her dress, threw another small log on the fire. He dressed, sitting down.

"Do you have to go?" he asked.

"Yes. I've already stayed too long."

"I'll miss you."

"I'm glad. I'll miss you too. I have to go into Oro City, tell them the meat will be there. It's important."

"I'm expecting a friend. He may be early. His name's Randall. Could you look him up, tell him where I am? Jed Randall. He'll be staying at the best hotel in town."

"That would be Alpine House. What's he look like?"

"Short, hair that won't tame, lightheaded, bowlegged. A cowboy."

"He'll stick out like a sore thumb."

Gunn laughed.

"Yes, Jed will. Anywhere."

They kissed. Stepped outside together. The flaps of the hide door rattled. It was solemn, white. The snow was not deep. The sun was already risen and would melt it to mud by afternoon. Gunn took a long breath, let it out.

"I should stay and fix you breakfast," she mused.

"You'd never get away if you did. Kristina, you do things to a man. Even when you don't do anything."

"You're sweet, Gunn. Walk with me to my horse?"

"I'll get my gear, eat on the hunt. If I eat. I like to hunt on an empty stomach."

Gunn saddled their horses, fed the mules, loaded his rifles, booted them on the rigging. Kristina rode away at a fast clip. At the edge of the trees, she looked back, waved. Gunn waved back and then turned Esquire in the opposite direction. He felt a tight pull at his gut and a churning inside. He missed her already.

A bad sign.

The game was easy to track, easy to see. The big elk and the mule deer were still in the high country, feeding late into the morning, scratching through the snow for grass. Their dropping steamed and, upwind, he smelled their musk long before he saw them. His rifles boomed and he gutted quickly. He hung the carcasses up to air, marked his path so he could bring the wagon, later.

He stopped a little after noon and chewed jerky, drank water. He wanted a hot meal, but the smell of smoke would carry a long way. It was harder to hunt, after that. The melting snow made Esquire slip and the game was bedded down. He jumped an eight point muley late in the afternoon, dropped him with a running shot. After that, it was quiet. He rode back to the corral, hitched up the team. It was dark before he finished hanging the meat from the cross-poles. He put the mules and his horse up for the night and staggered, dog-tired into the lean-to. He started a fire, made coffee, put on a skillet. He mixed beans and potatoes with the heart and liver of a bull elk. That was enough. The food would stick to his ribs.

He almost fell asleep while he smoked a last cigarette and watched the stars glisten in a cloudless sky. The temperature dropped sharply and his eyes grew heavy. He jammed the stove full of wood, crawled into his bedroll and listened to a lone wolf croon somewhere above timberline. He thought of Kristina and wondered where she was. He thought of Leni, too, and missed them both. It was dawn before he woke and he remembered no dreams.

Two days later, the wagon groaning under the weight of more than four thousand pounds of deer, elk and antelope, Gunn rode up to the cabin. He called out, rattled the traces.

Jed Randall, followed by Leni and Kristina, poured through the front door.

" 'Bout time you showed up," grinned Jed.

"What the hell you doin' here?"

"Just got in. Man, you shot some meat there."

"Some."

"Drive the wagon out back," said Kristina. "We're ready to start skinning."

"Welcome back," said Leni.

Gunn noticed that she had to force a smile. Something was wrong. Kristina, too, was subdued. He said nothing. Jed jumped up on the seat with him as he drove the team around the cabin. There were log tables pulled together. Gunn had never seen them before, but they had known much use. He realized that they had been covered with tarps and he just hadn't noticed them.

Jed helped Gunn unload the carcasses. They all started skinning, quartering. Kristina and Leni worked fast. The meat stacked up. They packed them in heavy crates, salted them down.

"Leni had some trouble while I was gone," said Kristina.

"I figgered," said Gunn. "Bad?"

"Bad," said Leni, her lips quivering. She told Gunn what had happened. Jed listened, with interest. Gunn's face hardened as he listened to the story of the break-in, marveled that Leni had handled herself so well. But, she would bear some scars, at that.

" 'Pears you have some enemies here yourself, Gunn," said Randall. "And, as usual, I got to pay the price."

"You might better explain that, Jed."

Jed told him about the run-in with Stagg's men. He didn't mention that Eloise Blake had befriended him. He sensed that Gunn had other things on his mind, maybe two things that were real important — Leni and Kristina. Kristina had found him in town, given him Gunn's message. He had waited a day before coming out because he had been talking to miners, riding the ridges, poking into dirt and rock looking for signs of silver. He had the fever bad. He didn't mention that either, at first.

"We'll run the meat into town tomorrow," said Kristina, her arms and hands bloodied from skinning. "Someone has to go to Denver. I don't know if we can spare you, Gunn. We need more. Ore City is running low on fresh meat."

"Jed, I'd like to hire you as a drover, if you're interested. Best the ladies take care of business and I've got to go back out."

Randall's face clouded.

"Dammit, Gunn, I . . ."

"Just yes or no, Jed. I'll pay you well."

"But, there's money to be made. There's silver, maybe gold. I've seen it, Gunn. I —"

114

Gunn fixed him with a look. It was very quiet. The women looked at Jed, then at Gunn. They stood like statues.

"Just yes or no, Jed."

The blizzard came without fair warning.

It came during the night, out of the north like some white-fanged demon, howling down over the glaciers in the high Rockes, whipping through the passes with the ferocity of sleet-laced winds, bringing in the snow. The wind blew the snow onto the ground with packing force as the storm front raged through the mountains. Then, the winds fell off, for a time, and the snow fell heavy, with a relentless monotony until the trees sagged under its weight, the passes closed up and the trails mounded up with drifts that looked like burial places for giants.

Gunn woke during the night, when the winds were singing under the eaves, when they howled against the shutters. He peered out into a black maelstrom of swirling snow. He shivered.

Jed grumbled in his bedroll on the floor.

Gun let him sleep, but he knew, from the sound of the storm, that he would not hunt the next day. Nor would the wagon get to Oro City. Unless he missed his guess, they would be snowbound. Perhaps, for days.

He dressed, went to the kitchen, lighted a lamp, put on a pot of coffee. Shrugging into his sheepskin coat, he went outside to check the horses and mules. His trouser legs soaked through, then froze, before he was through. When he returned, Kristina was sitting at the table in her robe, a steaming cup of coffee in front of her.

"It's bad out there, isn't it?" she said wearily.

"Yes. The stock's all right, though. The meat will freeze."

She got up, poured Gunn a cup of coffee. He had made it strong. There would be firewood to bring in when it was light.

They sat there, not speaking, for several moments. Finally, Kristina started talking. Her voice was whispery, low.

"I'm worried, Gunn. There are people in Oro City who are depending on the meat you brought in."

"I know."

"What can we do?"

"Nothing. Even if Jed had driven into town, he wouldn't have made it. That storm came up fast and my bet is the passes are closed. The wind made some big drifts. The wind will come up again in a day or so and finish off the job."

"There'll be men desperate for meat. There wasn't much left when I was in town yesterday."

"Can't be helped."

She started to cry, then. Gunn started to get up, but realized that she needed the release. She didn't cry very long and she looked fine after she dried her eyes. She gave him a wan smile.

"I'm sorry. I shouldn't let my emotions come up like that."

"You can't help what's happened. The weather is the weather."

"Stagg will make something of this, Gunn."

"I'll get the meat into town as soon as there's a break in the weather. Jed and I can probably make it if we get a decent day."

116

"People have been snowed in all winter up this high."

Gunn knew that. Their situation was not the best. They had plenty of supplies, but a meat shortage in a town like Oro City could be disastrous. Men would kill for a rabbit, a mouse, if they were starving. There was something about being snowbound too, that sent men over the edge. Nothing looked the same, nothing was the same. The whiteness, the bleakness, the knowing that one was cut off from the rest of civilization could drive one mad. He remembered the mining camps in Montana Territory, the importance of beef and vegetables during the hard winters. It would be the same here. A week of heavy snows could lock them in the cabin until late Spring.

Two women and two men in a small cabin could be a hardship by itself. Cabin fever. Being trapped.

"You got any snowshoes here?"

Kristina looked up at him, startled. The question had caught her by surprise.

"Yes. Three or four pair. Why?"

"Jed and I could pack a hundred, hundred and fifty pounds apiece, maybe, try to make it to Oro City."

"No!"

"If we could get the wagon in close enough, we might make several trips. Get some of the men in town to help."

Kristina thought about it a moment. Sipped her coffee. The silence stretched across the space between them. Finally, her eyes sparkled and she smiled.

"Yes, it could be done. It would be hard, but it could be done. Just that little bit of meat would help. But that would take days."

"Yes, but it's better than sitting around the cabin staring at each other, playing cards, wondering when one of us will go nuts."

"When would you try it?"

"In the morning. I doubt if the wagon would get very far, but it would be that much closer to town when we do get a thaw. We might even make some skis and get through."

"Did you ever ski?" she asked.

"No," he grinned. "I never showshoed before either. I try not to go anyplace my horse can't. But we can get some barrel staves or slats and try it if we need to."

"Gunn, you're a strange man. Why would you do all this for us?"

He didn't answer. He didn't know the answer. But whatever he would do would be for himself. He didn't like what Tolly's men had done to Randall. He didn't like what Tolly had tried to do with Leni. Yes, Stagg would take advantage of this situation. If he could. The trick was to check his moves, put him on the defensive. Even if they got some meat through, it would help. It would give the people in town some hope.

People could survive on hope.

CHAPTER TWELVE

Oro City looked as if someone had come through it during the night and whitewashed every building in town. It seemed caught in some ghostly light, frozen there, empty of people. But people were there, alive, beginning to stir. The clank of shovels and the startled voices of men began to rise on the morning air. The snow continued to fall; thick, wet, clinging.

"I make it four feet," said a grizzled oldtimer, peering through a window in the lobby of Alpine House.

"Easy," said another, in motheaten sweater, knit cap growing out of his eyebrows. "Maybe more."

"We'll be snowbound, fer certain sure."

The two men went to the dining room and ordered steak, eggs, bacon, biscuits and coffee.

But there was no steak. And there was no bacon.

The grumbling started and swept through the town by noon. By now, everyone knew that Lund was dead and another, a man named Gunn, was taking his place. Except he had not brought in any fresh meat. And the snow kept falling.

Tolly Stagg scraped a finger over his beard. The

bristles crackled with the sound.

There was a knock on the door of his hotel room.

"Come in," he said.

Reece Parker, Alf Suggs and Morton Brown crowded into the room. Brownie carried a hot pot of coffee and cups. Suggs had two full whiskey bottles in each hand. Packer threw some cigars on the table. Tolly looked away from the mirror, gestured.

"Take some chairs," he said. "We got talk to do. Pour that java, Brownie."

"It was noon and the snow had not let up. Some were predicting six feet of fresh stuff before nightfall.

Brownie poured the coffee. Suggs started to open one of the whiskey bottles. Tolly frowned, shook his head. He sat down, pulled a cup full of vaporing coffee towards him.

"No whiskey yet, Alf. I want to hear about this Gunn jasper."

Packer told him about Randy Coker, Cheyenne. Stagg listened, slurping his coffee, burning his tongue and lips. His eyes shifted from face to face, scanning his men, sizing them up once again. He wondered if they held Carp's death against him. He hadn't told them how it had happened. If they knew a young girl had stood him off, put Carp toes down, they'd think twice before they did what he wanted them to do. It was bad enough Carp was dead, but to think that little bitch had done it, stood up to him, backed him off, was a goddamned sorry state of affairs.

The room filled with the pall of blue smoke as the men puffed on cigars. The coffee went fast.

"This Gunn sounds like a real sidewinder," said Stagg. "I heard some tales, but never put much stock in 'em."

"He's real fast," said Brownie. "Had another thing he did what Packer didn't mention. Those men up in Wyoming. Good boys. Some we knowed. He shot 'em each three times."

"Huh?"

Tolly sat up straight, chewing hard on the cigar in his mouth.

"Yep. Each one. Three fuckin' times."

"So?" asked Stagg.

"They was all shot in the same place each time," said Brownie. Packer sat there, scowling, thinking.

"Same place?" Stagg leanded forward.

Brownie and Suggs looked at each other. Their faces paled. Packer coughed.

"What Brownie's tryin' to say," said Packer, "is that this was kind of a warning trademark this Gunn used. Somebody asked him about it one time, we heard and he said it was better'n usin' that brand. He shot those men in the head, heart and stomach. I saw one. Each shot clean; dead fuckin' center."

"That's just plain wasting lead," snorted Stagg.

"Mebbe so," admitted Packer, but they was a point to it. Gunn said he shot those men in the head, heart and belly to show people he meant business."

"Said they couldn't think, eat, nor love no more," added Brownie. "Give a man the shudders."

"Jesus Christ," said Tolly, "what kind of a bastard we got here?"

"A goddamned mean one," said Packer.

Eloise Black sighed, went back in the kitchen. She had managed to soothe everyone's feelings, but it couldn't last. There wasn't any beef, no game, no meat at all. She had sent a man all over town trying to buy what was left. No one had any meat to sell.

"We got plenty of firewood, Andy?" she asked a helper.

"Plenty," he said.

"You want me to work tonight Miss Blake?" asked the cook and round Mexican woman with crimson in her leathery bronze cheeks.

"People will want something. Potatoes, beans."

"There's no meat, though," said Andy, needlessly.

"I know it!" she snapped at him. She was immediately sorry. "Andy, forgive me. I'm just on edge. I need to think."

"You don't put much stock in this Gunn feller bringing in fresh game?" he asked. Andy Heathcock was a young swamper whose mother was a laundress. He was about twenty, freckle-faced, tow-headed. He was short, stocky, helped keep the kitchen clean, the wood for the stove piled up in the woodbox. He did other chores, as well. Eloise had come to rely on him. His father was dead, killed in a mining accident. He and his mother just barely got by. Andy had a point. She had never met Gunn and the more she heard about him, the more intrigued she was. But he was not a superman.

"I don't know, Andy. I doubt if anyone could get through in this storm. We'll just have to make do."

"There's Tolly Stagg. He's upstairs. In some meetin' with Packer and Suggs, that Brownie. He's been wantin' the meat contract anyways."

Eloise screwed up her face.

Andy had another point.

"He could maybe bring some meat in," said the

Mexican woman, whose name was Roberta Gonzales. "Even a little would help."

"Yes," said Eloise. "Perhaps you're right. I'll talk to Tolly. You say they're up in his room?"

"Two twenty two," said Andy, grinning. "Want me to go up there with you?"

"No. I can manage."

Eloise drew a breath, left the kitchen. She knew that Andy and Roberta were right. She had to do something. The meat shortage was already causing problems. Tolly might be able to hunt close to town, or get through to Denver. It was a long shot, but she owed her customers a try at getting meat. There was still time on Lund's contract, but if Gunn didn't get through soon. Today or tomorrow, she had little choice.

"So, this is our chance," said Tolly. "We hunt, best we can. Get some snowshoes, take along matches and tinder. Anything. Rabbits, quail, deer, elk, if we can find any. Take along a couple of scatterguns."

"It'll be pure hell huntin' in this goddamned weather," said Suggs. "Deer and elk have all gone to the flats."

"There's always some what stay behind," said Brownie.

The knock on the door interrupted their conversation."

"Who's there?" barked Stagg.

"Eloise Blake."

"Let her in, Brownie."

Eloise came into the room. She looked at Tolly, felt the heat of his eyes scorch her face.

"Do you think you can bring some fresh meat to

Oro City?" she asked, pointblank.

"Why Miss Blake," said Stagg with an exaggeration of politeness, "that's just what we aim to do."

"When and how much will it cost me?"

"Today, if we're lucky and the price we can figger out later."

The other men at the table snickered. Tolly's meaning was clear.

Eloise blanched.

"I am talking about hard coin, Mister Stagg."

"Why, so am I, Miss Blake," leered Tolly. "Real hard coin."

Gunn brought his fist down hard on the corral pole.

"Damn! Why didn't I think of that before? Jed, let's get some axes and a saw."

"You gone loco, Gunn?"

"Gunn's grey eyes flickered.

"Almost. Look, those women are longfaced and I almost let them down. I was thinking wrong. That meat has got to get to Oro City come hell or high water or a snowstorm. I was thinking of packing it in, sledding it in, skiing it in and probably busting my ass when the answer was there all the time. Right in front of me. Look up there, past those aspen. To the right. See them?"

Jed knit his brows, squinted. The snow was falling so thick he could barely see the base of the slope.

"All I see are a bunch of trees," he said glumly.

"Lodgepole pines, Jed. Perfect for making a travois. Two travois. Three, four." Gunn's elation failed to impress Randall. "Dig out some axes and a saw, meet you back here in a minute."

With that, Gunn tromped off through the thick snow, back into the cabin. Jed watched him go, shook his head and walked toward the tack room. They had been out there wondering how to break the meat apart, load it into packs if they had to—it was frozen solid in the crates. Now Gunn was talking about cutting down skinny pines and building Injun travois. That meant he was going to try and make it into Oro City, a long hard slog through thick snow.

Gunn called Kristina from the kitchen. He was buried under his coat and heavy mittens. Snow melted off his clothes and puddled on the floor.

"We're going to take that meat into town," he said, when she came into the room. "Can you and Leni stretch out those elk hides, start punching holes in them about six inches apart? Get some leather thongs or tough rope to string through them?"

"What are you aiming to do?"

"Build travois. Hook them to the mules and horses. We can pack near the whole load, I think. Better'n a sled, faster, maybe."

Her face lit up.

"That's a good idea, but we have tanned hides in one of the closets. They'd be better. Leni and I'll get right to work on it."

He kissed her, left her standing there. Before she could say anything, he had gone out the door, slammed it behind him.

They cut and trimmed eight long sturdy poles. Jed sawed the thick ends square, so that they had light poles. They lugged them down the slope, stacked them against the corral. Gunn brought out a mule and began rigging him up with harness. He found plenty of rope in the tackroom, cut it to fit. The travois poles would ride all right.

Afterwards, they lashed the cured hides to the dragging poles, making a trampoline to carry cargo.

"It's gonna work," said Jed.

"Damned right!" said Gunn, grinning. Leni and Kristina jumped out of pure joy to see the rig.

"Come on Jed, we got a lot of work to do." Gunn brought out another mule and harnessed him up. They worked fast. They did the same with Jed's horse and Esquire, so that they now could ride and lead the mules.

"I figure they'll carry the whole load," said Jed, when they were finished.

"Might," said Gunn, pleased. "We can hunt on the way, too. Kristina, we might fill your contract after all."

"Can we come?" asked Leni.

Gunn shook his head.

"No. It's going to be rough, but we ought to get through. It's thirty miles to Oro City and if we start out now, we'll have a good jump on getting there. But it means spending a night in the open. If it snows like it did last night, it could be bad for the horses and us."

"He's right, Leni. We'll wait for you Gunn. Good luck." Kristina bit her lip, turned away.

Jed stood there, banging his hands together to get them warm. The snow still fell steadily and the wind was starting to rise. It was past noon and thirty miles seemed like a million just then. He stomped his feet, watched his breath turn to smoke. The temperature was below freezing. The horses snorted, blew plumes of vapor from plastic nostrils, eyed him accusingly.

Gunn looked at Jed, shrugged.

"I'll be right back," he said.

Kristina stopped on the back porch, heard Gunn coming up behind her.

"You'd best go now," she said tightly. "I don't think . . ."

"Shut up," Gunn said, his voice low, confidential. "Go on inside."

She waited as he slammed the door.

"You're dripping all over the kitchen."

"It'll heal, Kristina. Don't make it any tougher on me."

She drew in a breath. Her breasts rose under her coat. He wanted her. She looked into his eyes and blinked, fighting back tears.

"Gunn, I didn't know this would happen to me. I . . ."

"You don't have to say anything. I know what it is."

"You do?"

"Yes."

"It hurts. All over. Deep inside."

"Yes. It hurts. It'll hurt all the time I'm gone from you. Dammit. Don't push it, Kristina. We can't look into the future."   .

"But . . . I want . . . I want . . ."

He went up to her, put a finger on her lips. He drew her close. Felt her breasts, soft, pliant, like over-ripe melons against his chest. He smelled her hair, looked at the smoothness of her face, wanted to crush her to him and never let her go. She put a hand on his sleeve, squeezed through the thick cloth and sheepskin of his coat. He felt a warmth flood his loins.

She felt him poking against her leg. Her eyes widened in stark surprise.

"You're quick," she breathed.

Even as she spoke, his manhood hardened to a steely shaft. He knew it was wrong to hold her like that, for so long, while Jed was standing in the cold, the horses and mules were waiting. He buried his muzzle in her hair and hated himself, but something surged in his heart. A tug, a grasping that took his breath away. A faint longing that had been buried in him for years rising to the surface. An ache in him he could not locate. A fragment of a dream suddenly real and unexplainable.

"Dammit," he said, his voice muffled in the tangles of her hair. "Dammit, Kristina, I . . ."

She pushed him away, stared at him with wide eyes. He drew a breath, held it.

"Gunn, don't say it. Not yet. Not if you don't know for sure. I know what's there. What's here. It may be animal. Physical. Lust, as the preacher would say. God, I know that's there. In me. In you. But . . . I don't want that to be why you lie with me, hold me. No, don't stop me. Don't say anything. What we have may grow, may make us happy or destroy us. I see that now. When you touch me, I melt inside. Like a candle dropped into a furnace. I've never felt like this before. I never expected to feel like this. Like the way I've felt. I—I just don't want to ruin it! Like I've ruined everything else . . ."

He started to say something, but Kristina threw herself back into his arms. He looked over her shoulder and saw Leni, quiet as a mourner at a funeral parlor slip into the room. His eyes smoked.

Kristina drew him close, hugged him tight and shuddered against him.

"I see," said Leni, loudly. "You shameless people! What am I? A post? A damned tree? Don't I have any feelings?"

Gunn's heart sank.

Kristina released him as if he had a plague. She whirled, facing her younger sister.

"Leni! How dare you say such things?"

"Kristina, you're nothing but a bitch! You knew he was mine! Oh, how could you?" She wailed, then turned, disappearing down the hallway. Gunn started to go after her.

Kristina pushed him back.

"No," she said, "this is something I must do. Leave Gunn. Leave now, before I can't bear it anymore."

"Krist . . ."

"Now!" she ordered.

Sheepishly, he turned away. There was so much he wanted to say to her. To Leni. But he was confused. He knew that. And there was no more time. Not if he was going to take the meat to Oro City. He walked out into the cold snowy air. A gust of wind struck him, burned his face like a furnace blast.

Jed Randall shot him a look from the corral fence where he had paced a path, packing the snow.

"Dammit, Gunn, we gonna leave or not? You wanta stay here and spark the ladies, I'll damn sure . . ."

"Shut up, Jed, damn you! Just shut your fuckin' mouth!"

Jed stood there. His jaw dropped.

And, finally, there was no more to say as the wind surged like a toothsome animal nibbling at their flesh.

The snow swirled down on the land, blotting the expressions on their faces, chilling their emotions.

They left, bent to the wind, riding their horses, leading the mules. The travois creaked under the weight of the meat boxes, the hides sagging, but holding firm.

The skies darkened and the tail of the storm threatened to be more merciless than its awesome front.

Gunn did not look back at the cabin, but ahead, to the monstrous drifts that seemed like impossible obstacles in his mind. The warmth he had felt with Kristina was gone, and in its place, a terrible cold that numbed him to the marrow of his bones.

CHAPTER THIRTEEN

The bugleing elk trotted back and forth, pacing a hardpacked path in the snow. Spumes of smokey breath issued from his nostrils. The young bulls and the cows milled together for warmth, watched the old bull flay the air with his antlers. The bowl-like valley was closed in by a snowslide, their exit to the low country blocked. Over six feet of snow deprived the animals of grass, and more was falling.

The bull stopped bugleing, froze.

His majestic rack held steady. His ears twitched. The herd stopped, too. A dozen heads lifted. Big eyes stared toward the pass.

Moments passed. Downwind, a man slid back out of sight.

"They's a herd up here all right, Tolly," said Suggs. "A dozen or so. Looks like you figgered right."

"We'll play hob gettin' 'em out," said Brownie. "Them drifts here are twenty feet deep."

Reece Packer scowled. The men looked like animated snowmen, their coats dusted with white as if they had fallen into a giant flour bin, their faces hidden behind scarves, hats tied down with kerchiefs to stay put in the gusting winds. Above the valley, sheer cliffs rose above timberline. There was only one way in and one way out. The big sled hooked up to a two-mule team teetered on the slope of a drift, its boxed sides holding in the falling snow. The mules filled the air with nasal steam. The men were cold and the animals shivered to keep their blood circulating. The air was thin at that altitude and it was hard to breathe. Brownie had coughed for the last five miles. Every breath he drew through his mouth seared his lungs. His nose was stuffed up and now his cheeks were raw from the wind, red as radishes.

"Mind you skin 'em quick before they freeze," said Stagg. "We'll circle 'em, move in. One man stays here, one goes around to the back of 'em. The other two come in from the sides, through the trees. They'll catch the upwind man's scent, so we'll move in slow while he gets in position. Reece, you ride to the far point. Brownie you take the left flank, I'll take the right. Alf, you set up here and shoot all you can. Fair enough?"

"Fair enough," chorused the men. Their horses were hip deep in snow now and the going would not be easy.

"Go on, Reece. You got the furthest to go," said Stagg.

Brownie rode off to the left, out of sight of the herd. Stagg followed Packer at a good distance. The men fought their horses through the drifts. Brownie had to circle a long way before he could find a way through to the trees on the other side of the snow-bound pass. It took most of an hour for the men to get into position. The snow was falling thickly, but the herd caught the scent of Packer and scrambled toward

Brownie's position.

Alf Suggs drove his horse up on top of the big drift's crest, rolling in the saddle as the animal wallowed through deep snow. His rifle barrel was so cold a bare hand would freeze to it. His hands felt like sausages inside his gloves and he held onto the stock where it was not so cold.

Tolly rode out of the trees as Packer came in at the rear of the herd. He picked a running cow at the head of the stampeding pack, led her, squeezed the trigger of the Sharps. The cow stumbled, staggered, went down on crumpled forelegs. Brownie emerged from the trees, began shooting. Packer shot from four hundred yards, brought down a young bull.

Suggs shot another bull and the herd swung away toward Brownie, toward the sheer rock face of the mountain. Brownie shot two and the herd turned again, scattered.

Reece moved in, picked out the old bull and fired his Winchester. The bullet struck the heart and lungs. The animal fell, rose, fell again. Reece rode up to him and fired a round into its brain. It quivered and thrashed, lay still. He was on it, cutting its throat, slashing into its hide to skin it out before it froze. Blood spattered the snow, crimson as trampled roses on a white sheet.

The men yelled and shot the herd to pieces. Not an animal escaped. The valley was littered with the carcasses.

The hunt, the kill, had been easy. Now, the hard work of skinning the animals out, hauling them over the snowdrifted pass and filling the box on the sled with meat, began. The minutes stretched into hours.

Suggs built a fire and the men ate half-raw livers and hearts to keep warm. Their hands turned wooden in the cold, elk blood froze to their mittens and clothes. Their faces turned ghostly with blown snow and the stone face of the mountain seemed to press down on them with a warning as the afternoon wore on. The shouts of exultation turned to curses, as they quartered the meat, carried it to the sled, or hauled sides of elk on hide sleds across the valley to the warming fire.

"We ain't gonna make it out of here tonight," said Brownie, his teeth chattering like seeds in a gourd.

Tolly looked at the darkening snow and nodded.

"Better start looking for a shelter," said Stagg. "Up next to the rock wall where the snow ain't so deep."

And the darkness continued to creep over the land as the snow piled up another half a foot.

They built another fire, worked until they could no longer see.

Then, the wolves came.

Gunn squinted, his eyes stung by the lashing wind. He was half-blind from the endless whiteness. At times, he felt as if he was walled in, lost. The travois poles cut deep and the ruts filled in with snow behind them so that when he looked back all he could see was blankness as if they had never moved as if they were going nowhere into a bottomless white abyss.

Jed Randall jerked the reins, pulling the recalcitrant mule through an eight foot drift. He had only been this way once and now the landmarks were blotted out, invisible. He had lost all sense of direction and was blindly following Gunn who knew the ways of shadows on snow, so faint a man could only sense their existence if he was smart enough, keen enough. The snow had a cast to it, he knew, but few men could read it. For him, there were no shadows, no pearly laquers on the fallen flakes. There was only the brainless whiteness, the small space that suffocated him as the wind ragged at his face, tore at his eyes, and the snow, maddeningly monotonous, without surcease, drifting from the sky in sheeted veils.

"Damn you, Gunn! You made of iron? Jesus! We're getting chawed to pieces by this damned wind!"

Gunn turned, looked at Randall, grinned. He pointed to an expanse of whiteness on the snow.

"Birds," he said.

"Huh?" Randall's mouth opened and his word was torn out of his mouth by a sudden gust of snowscurry wind.

Gunn reined up.

"Quail," he said. "Get your scattergun out."

"Are you plumb loco?"

The grin on Gunn's face was obliterated by a swirl of snow. He reached for his left scabbard, drew the shotgun from its sheath. He dismounted, wrapped the mule's rope around a stirrup, tied his own reins to a tree. He cracked the double barrel, slipped in two shotshells. Randall took his time, but Gunn doubled back to where he had seen the quail's tracks.

"Damn, Gunn," said Randall, panting as he caught up to Gunn. "We hunting quail in ten feet of snow?"

"They should be holed up. I figure they were roosting in trees until the wind blew them out. Might make a nice supper. Give us some strength in case we have more weather."

"More weather?" Ain't this a damned 'nough?"

Gunn motioned for Jed to fan out to his left as he followed the tracks. It was a small covey, less than a dozen. Their birdfeet crisscrossed in the snow, were fast filling up. They must have passed no more than minutes before. Gunn took his steps careful, cautioned, through sign language, for Randall to do the same.

He carried the Baker over-and-under, eased the hammer back on the bottom barrel. Randall carried a double-barrelled twelve gauge with the barrels sawed off to 18 inches. The wet of the snow clung to their legs and boots. The quail tracks led into a thicket. Gunn motioned for Randall to circle it. Gunn went the other way.

Randall, on the other side, shook his head. Gunn caught up to him. No tracks had come out of the thicket. There had to be a dozen birds or so holed up out of the wind.

"Cover me, Jed. Try for a double."

Jed nodded, shivering. He removed a glove, cocked both barrels of the shotgun. Gunn walked up to the thicket, kicked it. Three birds rattled out of the bushes. Two angled away from Jed toward the thick woods, the single went high just past Gunn. He fired, dropping it. Jed's shotgun boomed. The air was filled with feathers. Gunn reloaded fast as more birds boiled out of the thicket. He heard Jed's shotgun fire again, twice. Gunn shot his second bird as it reached the top of its rise, tried to level off. It was an easy shot. More birds flew out as he was reloading, but Gunn let them go.

They picked up six birds. Jed had gotten a double

with one shot.

"You'll appreciate this tonight," said Gunn, gutting them quickly with his Mexican knife. He put the birds inside his shirt around the top of his beltline to keep them warm.

"I'm froze up bad, Gunn. How much longer we going to go on?"

The storm was bad. Gunn knew that. The wind stung his eyes. The quail's blood was already obliterated on the snow and whatever tracks they had made were long since gone.

"Ride until the light starts to fail, then we'll hole up, build a fire."

"Fair enough. You know we could get lost real easy in this shit."

"It's been done. I've heard of men, women, too, getting caught in such a blizzard right near their homes. Never made it back. Some were found a few feet or inches from their door, froze to death."

"Godamn! Don't tell me stories like that."

Gunn said something, but his words were snatched away by the wind. They had to bend forward to reach the horses. The mules were packed so close they had to kick them away to mount up.

The grey-eyed man took his bearings and led the way, Jed following. There were places where the wind had swept the snow away from the road, showed the cuts in the hillside. He knew he was headed right, but the road wound around the mountains and there were places that were treacherous. Dangerous footings were hidden under drifted snow that could give way with a horse's weight. Gunn chose his way carefully. He had to stop and check with Randall several times. Jed had been this way before, Gunn had not.

Once, Esquire got stuck in a big drift and Gunn was panting by the time he hauled him out. He had to dismount, shovel with his hands and then pull the animal out of the heavy drift. His hands and arms were almost frozen. He whacked them against his legs, flexed his fingers inside sodden gloves. By early afternoon they had made but a few miles. The horses and mules were foundering every few yards.

The wind continued to howl and the snow accumulated at an alarming rate. Finally, Gunn knew that they could go on no longer. His mind was beginning to numb. He began to see things that were not there: a railroad car, a locomotive, an Indian waving a blanket, a cabin in the woods, with smoke curling from its chimney. His eyes burned in their sockets, his mouth dried up from exertion. His toes ached with the cold. His fingers burned as if he had held them in a fire until the flesh peeled back.

"Jed, we've got to find shelter, get a fire going before my hands won't work anymore."

"Yair, Gunn. I don't know if I can hold a match."

"Any ideas?"

"Find a deadfall, crawl under it."

"Be lucky to do that."

"An overhang, even a big tree."

"We'll look for some spruce growing close together. Have to leave the road."

"Hell," said Randall, "I ain't seen the road all godamned day."

It was true. They might be on the road or they might not. Gunn didn't know. He didn't even know if he was heading for Oro City anymore. But he said nothing to Jed. No use in both of them being lost.

They found some blue spruce on a flat, three of them growing close together. They rode up to it after what seemed like hours of making no headway, and rode into the shelter. At least the wind did not tear at their eyes like shaven onions and there was a semblance of warmth. Neither man realized that their hell was just beginning.

CHAPTER FOURTEEN

Gunn knew they had to work fast, or die.

They unlashed the travois, used the poles to rig a shelter for the horses. Jed cut spruce bows for a roof, while Gunn roamed the woods in search of deadwood for a fire. It was brutal slogging through the drifts that were sometimes waist-high. He cut wood with deadened hands and fingers that responded only with the sheer effort of his will. He started a fire and hoped it would melt the snow enough so they'd have a place to put their bedrolls. Then, he gathered more wood, even though he wanted only to lie down and sleep, an act he knew would be fatal.

There was no sky and no land. Only the trees and the animals had any definition. The snow fell with such monotonous insistence that their senses were blocked off. They felt trapped, locked in. The fire sputtered and crackled. Clumps of snow fell from the spruce and dampened the flames. Jed huddled next to it on bended knees, nurturing it, warming his frosted hands that tingled with pain as the heat penetrated the flesh. Gunn staggered in and out of the makeshift shelter, his clothes saturated with snow, his face a frozen mask.

"I'll spell you, pardner," Jed said. "Get warm some."

Gunn collapsed next to the fire, his brain stunned by the cold at his extremities. He lay there, gazing at the flames, wondering when the heat would hit. He saw Randall pick up the axe and duck under the feathered branches of the blue spruce, disappear into a whirling world of windwhipped snow. He dozed, then cringed in pain as the fire shot through half-gelid flesh clear to the bone. He winced, and tears boiled in his eyes.

When he could stand the pain enough to move his fingers, he dug into his shirt for the quail. He plucked them, holding them close to the fire, tossing their feathers into the flames, watching them burn, fascinated by the way the torchfingers consumed them. The singed feathers stung his nostrils. He rubbed the fine hairs from their delicate bodies and packed their gutted insides with snow that melted as he laid them close to the fire.

Where the snow had melted, there was a layer of mud. Gunn scooped up the mud and dabbed it on the quail bodies, building it up to a thickness of half a thumb. Then he shoved the mudcased quail into the base of the fire. Feeling returned to his fingers, but his toes were still numb with cold.

They took turns bringing in firewood until the darkness came on them. Jed brought out a coffee pot, filled it with snow, melted enough to make a pot of coffee, filled it with ground beans. The cold had taken away their appetite, but they both knew they would need nourishment. Gunn dug the quail out of the fire with his knife and cracked the mud open. The quail were baked, steaming. He tossed one to Jed who devoured it hungrily. The wind howled, sought them out in their meager shelter, but they each ate three quail. Gunn gave up trying to light a cigarette. Instead, he had Jed help him move the fire. It almost spluttered out until they built it back up, but they had a small place for their bedrolls that was hot from where the fire had been. They could at least put their feet on warm ground, their heads closer to the fire.

Gunn stacked firewood behind the fire to act as a reflector and the men turned in, exhausted, one on either side of the fire.

"We might freeze before mornin'," said Randall.

"At least that would stop the noise, the pain."

"Yeah, I reckon."

"Good night, Jed."

"Night, Gunn."

The fire burned down fast, went out some time after they fell asleep. The embers continued to glow, but the wind blew them to grey coals and scattered them into the drifting snow. The bedrolls mounded with more snow, blanketing the sleeping men with a deadly warmth.

The screaming horse woke Gunn first.

He jerked the blanket from his head and blinked into the pitch darkness. The horses both screamed and the mules brayed with a bloodcurdling sound. Gunn struggled to throw off his blankets, realized he was buried in snow. It was a wonder to him that he hadn't suffocated to death.

He grabbed up his gunbelt in the dark, husked commands at Randall. He sought a rifle, trying to remember which underside of the bedroll he had stashed his Winchester. Lund's shot had left a depression in the receiver and he felt for it now.

"Jed, dammit, get up."

He heard a muffled voice, saw a mound stir now that his eyes were adjusted to the dark, the expanse of white snow that was the only source of light, of definition. The spruce trees loomed around him, like a giant circular wall.

"Huh?"

"Get your ass up, Jed. We got to get to the horses."

There was a rustling sound, a flurry of snow tossed in the air as Randall climbed out of his bed.

"What's goin' on?"

"Wolves. Or a bear."

Gunn didn't wait for Jed, but fought his way under the spruce bows and waded through hip-deep snow toward the shelter they had made for the stock. He heard them now. The wolves, baying and snarling, teeth snapping. He wished he had a torch, a lantern. It was black as a cave and his face felt the cobwebby flakes of snow as they tinked against his skin and melted or clung to his beard stubble. He drew his Colt and fired a round into the air.

The horses screamed. The wolves fell silent, except for their muttered snarlings.

Where the hell was Jed?

Gunn drew close, felt something brush against his leg. His nostrils filled with the stench of wolf. He saw something out of the corner of his eye, wheeled, and saw no target. Only an empty pit of blackness, the impression of falling snow. He foundered in the drifts, buried the Winchester as he fell headlong. His hands started to freeze up.

He fired another shot into the air above his head.

The mules bleated with asthmatic wheezing, and the horses neighed hysterically.

Something dove through the blackness at Gunn's throat.

He felt the rush of air, smelled the fetid stale breath. He ducked, instinctively, and the animal struck him, knocking him backwards. He fell into a mound of snow, sank like a stone in a stack of feathers. Snarling animals surrounded him, sniffed him, bit at him, as he flailed his arms, struggling to get to his feet.

Where in the holy Christ was Randall?

He heard a shot, saw orange flame belch from the barrel of a rifle. For a split second his surroundings were illuminated by the brief flash. A wolf yelped and he saw one twist and leap into the air. The rifle boomed again and he heard the bullet thunk into flesh. He sat up, drew his pistol, fired at a dark shape close by. Something furry hit him in the chest. He brushed it aside as if it was a mass of cobwebs. The flash from his pistol had illuminated still another target. His eyes adjusted to the light. He fired again, two shots quickly snapped off and the wolves yapped in pain.

Jed Randall swung his rifle like a club at a leaping wolf, heard bone crunch as the rifle butt struck its skull.

Gunn emptied his pistol and it was quiet.

Above them, they heard distant rifle fire, sounding like ghostly echoes in the silence of the falling snow.

"Did you hear it?" asked Packer? Down below, on the road."

"Yeah," said Tolly Stagg, weary beyond caring. "The damned wolves are everywhere tonight."

"That means someone's headed for town. Maybe that Gunn with fresh meat."

They had shot wolves by firelight for over an hour, it seemed. The snow was strewn with the freezing carcasses, the dead fur thickening with snowflakes. The wind continued to keen, burning their ears, frosting their faces.

"Tell Brownie to stand the last watch, wake us before first light," said Stagg.

"We ought to go down there, take care of them," said Packer.

"Likely we'll run into 'em. We got to take the road too."

"I'll be ready," said Reece, bending into the wind, heading for Brownie's position on the other side of the fire. The snow gleamed pearly in the firelight, danced with shadows. On a ridge below, a wolf howled and his cry was swallowed by the wind.

Alf Suggs shivered at his post beyond the firelight, resting on his long circular walk, his mind as frozen as his hands. He saw things that were not there and every shadow was a snarling, fanged wolf, ready to leap at him. His clothes were covered with blood, from skinning, from a wolf that he had shot four inches from his throat.

The game had gone and the wolves had stayed too long in the high country. They were hungry, but had found other game down below. Even as he listened, the firing stopped and it was quiet again.

But the shadows were still there as he began walking his post again.

Kristina added another log to the fire, curled back up in the chair. She couldn't sleep, not with the wind howling and the cabin creaking with a thousand startling sounds. She missed her father, Gunn. She thought of him out there somewhere, perhaps freezing to death. Twice, she and Leni, had had to go out with lanterns and shoot at wolves, wolves that had come down and tried to get at the horses. They had killed one and the others had torn it to pieces, leaving the snow spattered with blood. Leni was at the back window now, listening, in case they returned.

She wished now she had just relinquished her father's business. Sold it to Tolly Stagg, or given it to him. Now, two men were in peril because of her own stubborness. One, she scarcely knew, the other . . . could she be in love with him? She thought of his strong arms, his broad shoulders, his wide deep chest. Thought of him naked against her, his loins hot.

Her eyelids dipped. The fire drew on her strength, made her sleepy. The crackling sounds soothed her troubled mind.

Leni startled her when she walked quietly into the room.

"You asleep?"

"Leni! You scared me. I—I was dozing."

"I—I think they've gone away. The wolves."

"Yes, sit down, keep me company."

"I'm not very sleepy yet. I keep wondering how Gunn is, and Jed, too."

"Me too. You like him, don't you? Gunn, I mean."

"You know I do."

"So do I."

Leni sighed, sat down on the divan, leaned toward the fire. Her eyes danced with light.

"We can't both have him," she said softly.

"No. I doubt if either of us can."

"What do you mean?"

Kristina stretched her legs, shifted her position. She looked at her little sister with sympathy.

"Because he's not the kind to settle down. Not yet. He's half-wild and I guess his wife's death had something to do with that."

"He told you about it," Leni said quickly, stung with a sudden jealousy.

"A little. When I asked him."

"You made love with him, didn't you?"

"Let's not fight. I don't know how long this man will stay around, but if we fight over him, it won't be long."

Leni let the silence linger, fill up the room. She tried to reason as Kristina did, but she could only think of what she had had one night, a night she couldn't forget. It surprised her that Kristina had been with him — her sister had always seemed above falling for a man. But Gunn was someone special. He had something that attracted women. That, too, made her jealous. But she wanted Gunn, despite what her sister said. She meant to fight for him.

"I'm going to bed," said Leni. "Are you going to stay up?"

"No . . . no, I'm sleepy now." Leni came out of her chair, threw more wood on the fire, enough, she hoped to last until morning. "Leni, we might saddle up and try to ride to town, see if the men are all right. If it stops snowing."

Leni's face brightened.

"Oh, do you think we could?"

"I miss him too, hon. Terribly."

Leni, softened, went to Kristina threw her arms around her. Kristina returned the embrace.

"I love him," said Leni. "I can't bear to think of anything happening to him."

"I know, little sister. Don't worry. He'll be all right."

But she wondered. When the contract was filled, she wondered if they would ever see Gunn again.

CHAPTER FIFTEEN

Gunn stared at the half-eaten wolf carcasses.

The snow had stopped falling sometime during the night and the wind had died down to a few feeble gusts. Now, in the gray half-light of morning, he inspected the scene of horror from the night before. The horses and mules had come through it all right. A dead wolf, its neck broken, lay trampled in the makeshift shelter. Snow had drifted high against the poles and they were iced in, but a few hits with an axe ought to free them. The game meat was intact.

Jed came up behind him, carrying tin cupsful of steaming coffee. He handed one to Gunn.

"Road looks okay in spots," said Randall. "We ought to get through unless there was a landslide."

"We could get caught in one if that sun comes up."

Jed peered into the sky, sipped his coffee.

"It's trying to, I reckon."

"Best finish our coffee and get to it."

"Yair. First night I spent that lasted pert near a week."

"You got a long morning ahead of you, son."

The men drank their coffee in silence, the heat giving them the illusion of warmth. It was still cold.

The horses and mules were restless. They didn't like the smell of wolves—dead or alive.

In a little over an hour, they had broken free of the drifts, were on the road, the travois scraping ruts through the frozen crust. The sun was only a pale light behind high thick clouds. Occasionally a flurry of snow fell. Jed led the way now, squinting against the unaccustomed brightness of light reflection off the mica-like sheen glazing the surface of the snow. They passed by steep slopes, felt the weight of thick packed snow above them, jerked the mules past three dangerous places, trying to make as little noise as possible. A sound could trigger an avalanche, sweep them away with no trace until Spring.

Esquire twitched his ears, balked. He tossed his head, snorted. His mane rustled in the dry winter air.

Gunn instinctively ducked, then slid half out of the saddle in the direction opposite to where the horse was staring. The lazy sound of a shot drifted to his ears, and he heard the hackle-raising sizzle of the bullet as it passed close by. He clawed for his pistol, gripped the saddle horn, swung his right leg over the horse's rump.

"Watch it, Jed!" he called.

A second shot close after the first.

Randall spilled out of the saddle, as the bullet whined where he had been. He wrenched his shoulder when he hit, knew that if he had not jumped he would have packed extra led in his hide. He saw the smoke puff from the ridge. It lingered in the air, then spread slowly, mingling with the grey clouds and white snow until it was hard to see.

"Goddamn!" he exclaimed.

Gunn saw the smoke puff too, and threw his pistol over Esquire's neck, cocking the Colt. He squeezed off a shot, aiming high to allow for the terrible drop. The distance was great; a rifle shot, really, but at least he was answering the deadly challenge. He saw movement. A hat. He cursed, slid from his stirrup. He would be exposed on the other side, but he had to jerk the Winchester free of its boot.

Another shot cracked.

A spurt of snow kicked up inches from Randall's head.

Gunn moved quickly, stood up, snatching the Winchester free of the scabbard. He slid back to the other side of his horse.

Whoever was up there was a deadly shot. He meant business. The last round had plowed a furrow in the snow inches from Jed's face, spattering him with churned up flakes.

Jed rolled, drew his pistol.

"Take cover!" Gunn growled.

Randall rolled off the road, snugged himself against a snowbank. A bullet followed him, smacking into the snow seconds after he moved. He felt a lump rise up in his throat.

Gunn crabwalked back to Esquire's rear, cocked the Winchester. The shell slid into the chamber; the hammer cocked back. He brought the rifle to his shoulder, took aim. He saw a hat bobbing on the ridge. He allowed for the drop, sucked in his breath. He steadied, held his breath. He squeezed the trigger almost tenderly.

There was no way of telling if his aim was true. He waited, listening for a yell, a scream.

There was nothing.

The seconds ticked by, slow, empty.

"What do ya think?" asked Randall.

Before Gunn could reply, another shot ripped the silence. Snow spattered against Esquire's leg. The horse backed up.

"Whoa, boy," said Gunn. "I think, Jed, our boy's still up there. He's got us pinned down."

"Who in hell is it?"

Gunn shrugged, looked up at the ridge. The hat, or something, was still there. They couldn't stay in the open like this. The rifleman may have wanted to keep them there until more muscle arrived.

"You cover me, Jed. I'm going to circle him, try and come up from behind. If I can make it to that big Spruce, I might be able to keep from getting shot the rest of the way up. Way up there, above that bastard's a scrub pine'll give me good cover once I'm up there. I can set up there, break his back with a rifle shot. Figure the shot's no more'n a hundred fifty yards from there."

"That'll take a hour, at least."

"Yeah. Or we could stay here here and freeze our balls off and let him shoot us to pieces."

"I'll cover you," said Randall.

Gunn steeled himself for the run to the big Spruce tree, standing on the slope about fifty yards from his position. He fired a shot at the ridge, then ran, bent over. Jed fired three shots before Gunn reached the tree. He leaned against it, panting. A report from the ridge, made his blood freeze. A bullet thunked into the tree, sent showers of slivers past his face.

"The bastard," Gunn muttered.

Jed answered with two more shots.

Gunn floundered through deep snow to the next tree, but he was already out of sight of the ridge. From here on he would be traveling blind. If the ambusher came to meet him, he would have the advantage of higher ground. Gunn decided to take that advantage away.

He tried to get up the slope fast, but the snow was too deep. He was tiring fast and the cold was numbing his feet, hammering at his legs. He had to criss-cross, back and forth. It was slow going.

But no one shot at him.

He found some places where the wind had scoured the slopes, left him icy, but firmer footing. He made good time on these places, finally reached the ridge.

Cautiously, he made his way from the tree to tree, rifle cocked and ready. He lungs burned at that altitude. The snow dazzled him, blinded him when he looked at it for too long. He heard no more shots and stillness made him wonder if the man on the ridge wasn't circling him or Jed. It was eerie up there, unable to see Jed, uncertain of where bushwacker was—or had been. But Gunn kept a ridge between himself and the ambusher's position, just to be sure. A jay swore at him and Gunn froze against a lean pine, listening. Waiting for the shot that never came.

A gnarled pine, blistered bare by the grit and teeth of strong winds stood on knoll overlooking the place where the ambusher had waited for them. This was the scrub pine Gunn had spotted from below. He knew where he was. He knew where the bushwacker ought to be.

He looked around. The wind blew hard here and

153

the ground was swept bare in spots. If there had been tracks here, they were gone now. He ran a zig-zag pattern toward the tree. Nobody shot at him. He waited until his breathing returned to normal, then hunkered low at the thickest part of the tree's trunk. He peered at the spot where the ambusher had fired at them.

There was no one there!

Instead, a man's hat lay where he had seen it, shoved into the snow so it wouldn't blow away.

Gunn cursed softly to himself.

He scrambled down the slope, picked up the hat. Jed, atop his horse, leading Esquire rode out of a grove of trees. Gunn looked at him in surprise.

"Figgered you might want to ride down," said Randall.

"You saw him leave?"

Jed nodded.

"Out of range, about a half hour ago. He knew what he was doing."

"The sonofabitch."

"Yair."

Gunn drew a breath. His lips tightened together. A muscle twitched in his cheek. His blue-grey eyes flickered with a dangerous light, narrowed as he assessed the situation. He took the reins Jed offered, walked up to the left stirrup. He pulled himself into the saddle, shoved the Winchester into its scabbard. Esquire shifted his hooves, stood hipshot.

"He wanted us to lose some time here," Gunn said, finally. "Why? There's just one man's tracks up here." Thinking out loud, he looked down where the mules were. "He could see us plain. Given enough time,

154

maybe, he could have killed us. Could have shot our horses, the mules."

"Bad shot?"

"No. A good shot. He got cold, went on. But he was here for a reason. To slow us down. Why, dammit why?"

Jed hunched down inside his coat, pulled his collar up to keep out the wind. He said nothing.

"Stagg," decided Gunn. "One of his bunch. They must be heading for Oro City. Maybe he means to cut us out of the meat business."

Jed's face lit up.

"Sounds like you got it, Gunn."

"We'll see what we pick up on the trail. My hunch is right, there'll be a sign. Come on, let's get the mules and get to it."

There was a sign.

The lone rider had caught up to the others a good ways down the road. Deep dark holes in the snow told Gunn that there were four men, at least, and they were pulling a sled that was heavy-laden. The deep ruts showed him that much and more.

"They're making good time. I'd say it took the bushwhacker almost an hour to catch up. You can see where they brought the sled in out of that canyon. They must have a hell of a time getting up there. But they brought home the bacon. Ruts are filled in enough to give me some idea." Gunn checked their own tracks, estimated the time it would take to match them up to the ones left from the men pulling the sled. "I give them two hours, hour and a half, maybe. More like two hours. And, they're traveling some faster. How much farther to Oro City, Jed?"

"Ten mile, maybe a shade less."

Gunn swore.

"They'll beat us in."

"I reckon. With that much of a start."

Gunn touched the hat inside his coat. The one the bushwacker had left up on the ridge. There were four men, at least, he would have to face. But he wanted the one who fit that hat. He wanted him bad.

"Come on, Jed, let's see how fucking close we can make it."

Reece Packer panted for breath. He had four bandannas tied under his chin, covering his ears, but they were still cold. The top of his head was frozen. Tolly Stagg tried not to laugh every time he looked at Packer. He rattled the reins over the team's back, shifted his weight on the sled's seat. The buffalo robe on the seat made him feel the cold less intensely, but it was no Sunday picnic. The mules were tiring and they had ways to go. A hard ways to go.

"I owe you a new hat, Reece."

"Onliest thing to do. That Gunn's a damned blood-hound. He come after me like fire after dry brush."

"You gave us time. Obliged."

"I tried to kill him, Tolly. But it was damned cold up there. Hard to see with the wind blowin' square in my eyes."

"Don't worry about it."

"He'll keep comin', that one," said Reece, dropping back as his horse slid into a drift. The road was getting worse, it seemed. They were not making the progress they had been and there was a stretch ahead that was open with a long steep slope bordering the road. Prime avalanche country. Alf Suggs was breaking trail and Brownie was trying his best to widen it some.

Tolly thought about what Reece had said. He'd have to take care of Gunn. He was the only one standing in his way. There might be a way to eliminate him and rustle his meat at the same time. No use working for it, he reasoned, if it could be took. They were about an hour's going from Oro City. If he could beat Gunn in, deliver the elk meat, then he might still have time to take Gunn and Randall out before they came over the hill.

Stagg clucked to the team, but they didn't respond. Heads down, they took slow steps through deep snow as the sled slid over the snow, sank into it, dragged at their remaining strength.

CHAPTER SIXTEEN

The sled and the other riders in Stagg's bunch packed the snow and made the going easier for Gunn and Randall. The two men followed the packed trail, began to gain on the Stagg riders ahead of them. For the past several minutes, Gunn had noticed a change in the tracks. They were clearer now, etched more sharply. The tracks had not filled in so much.

"We might give them a race at that," said Gunn, turning in his saddle. "That sled is dragging to beat hell."

"So I noticed. No chance of stopping, building a fire, I reckon."

"No chance," said Gunn tersely.

Kristina could hardly move in the heavy clothing she wore. She looked at Leni and laughed. Leni looked like a giant bug, with only a small portion of her face showing out from under the scarves and hat she wore. They both had on two pairs of heavy woolen socks and itched from woolen underwear.

"Are you ready?" Kristina asked her sister.

Leni gave her cinch one more tug, slipped the tongue through the hole. She grunted, waddled to her horse's head, picked up the reins in hands that wore doubled gloves.

Kristina laughed aloud.

"What's so funny?"

"You. Me. I wonder if we can even get in our saddle."

Leni chuckled.

"You look like a bear," she said.

Kristina grabbed her saddle horn, stuck a clumsy foot in the stirrup. With a tug, she pulled herself up, managed to throw a leg over the cantle. Leni followed suit. They were leaving late, but there had been a lot to do and the decision to ride to Oro City had been considered and reconsidered a dozen times. But they were going, at last. They dreaded the ride, what they might find after the storm of the night before.

It was almost noon.

Tolly Stagg hauled in hard on the reins.

The road was blocked. Snow lay heaped in front of them, where a talus slope had given way. The avalanche had ripped out trees, overturned boulders, killed at least one deer. Its twisted carcass jutted out from a snowbank, antlers shredded and splintered.

"Gawdamn!" exclaimed Brownie.

"We're blocked for fair," muttered Suggs. "Dammit, Tolly, we can't go around it and it's ten hunnert feet down the other way."

Tolly was worried. They had been making slow time. The sled had been bottoming out, piling up snow so much they'd had to shift the load of elk meat, help the team pull it. The sled was snowplowing. The runners needed to be greased with tallow, and there was no time to stop, unload, jack the sled up and take care of this business. The snow, from friction, was melting and icing back up so that the runners thickened, grew heavier, lost traction as they sank through the crust into powder.

He turned to Packer, his eyebrows rising in questioning arcs.

"How much time we got, Reece? Before those bastards catch up to us?"

"Not much, Tolly. The hour or so we gained is lost. They're hauling travvies and probably riding over the trail better'n us."

Stagg heaved air from his chest, stood up to stretch.

"The fuckin' cold," he said. "That goddamned snow. You thinkin' what I'm thinkin'?"

"Dynamite?"

"Yeah, Reece. I got four sticks. You?"

"A couple, some caps, fuses. Have to place 'em right."

"See if Brownie'n Alf have some sticks. We need to get some of that snow out of the way."

Packer looked at the slope. The high ground. There was no way of knowing how much snow was up there. Plenty. A blast could bring it all down on them, make it worse. He was a powderman himself, but he'd never worked in snow before. He could cut a stick, rig a row to blast a road or tunnel through rock, but this was scary. Damned scary. In this country a man carried dynamite as a matter of course. It was always useful. There was so damned much rock. It was also a very persuasive weapon at times. There was no telling how stable it was now, though, with the cold and the age of the sticks. He'd had these in his saddlebags for months. All summer, at least.

"Brownie, Alf! You got any sticks in your packs?"

Brownie stood up in the stirrups, nodded. Alf started rummaging through a worn saddlebag, twisting in the saddle until his back hurt. He found two sticks wrapped in yellowed pages of the Rocky Mountain News.

"I got four sticks," said Brownie, a box of caps, some fuse."

Alf Suggs held up the two sticks in a gloved hand.

"Well?" asked Stagg of Packer.

"We can maybe do some good. But you got to be ready to run it."

"Meaning?"

"Meaning that whole fuckin' mountain's liable to come down on us. You got to back up the sled, too."

"Jesus shit Christ!" exclaimed Stagg.

"No tellin' what'll come up. I'll halve the sticks, set 'em a foot apart. Rig both sides of the road. Hell, they's twelve foot of snow smack dab in front of us, Tolly."

"Set it, then. Time's a-wastin'."

They backed the sled down. Tolly checked the runners while Reece and the others cut the dynamite sticks in half, set them in rows wide enough to let them pass. Packer shoved caps in each stick, into the packed sawdust, the gelatin. He worked with bare hands. The dynamite itself, sawdust and gelatin laced with nitroglycerin, was pretty safe to handle. But the powerful caps could blow a man's hand or arm off if exploded. He would have liked to have had at least a box of dynamite, set the half-sticks no more than four inches apart, but he had to make do with what he had. The trick was to fuse only the lead stick and hope the explosion was strong enough to set off the other caps. So, the sticks had to be close enough for the initial blast to do that. There were other problems as well.

The sticks had to be set low enough to do any good. That meant that they would have to dig grooves through the snow. There was also the matter of getting out of the way, behind something big and thick and heavy. A rock or a tree stump could take a man's head off. Stones would be like bullets, like grapeshot. The concussion could blow a man's ear drums out, give him a permanent ringing in the ears.

"Need two trenches dug through that snow," said Reece, measuring his fuse. The fuse was fast-burning, the time measured in inches and seconds. He made it long. "And make sure you set 'em wide enough for that sled to get through."

Tolly came up, on foot, watched Alf cut through the dynamite sticks with a skinning knife.

"Save one stick, Alf," said Stagg.

"How come?" asked Packer. "We'll need 'em all. Need two dozen more, in fact."

"We may need one. Cap it an fuse it." He looked at Reece with slitted eyes.

Reece understood. He looked down the backtrail briefly, nodded. If Gunn came up on them, a stick of nitro would discourage a whole hell of a lot of attention from the man. It could be an ace in the hole in other ways as well.

Tolly walked back to the shed, kicked the runners all around. He didn't want them freezing to the snow. When the time came, the sled had to move. Now two ways about it. It had to move through the blasted-out snow and not stop until Oro City.

The brightness blistered Gunn's eyes, so that he had to turn away from it and look at his horse's neck and mane. His eyes burned like coals in their sockets. The trail blurred, the sled marks widened and converged as if they were actually moving. The deep hoof prints moved like black dots up and down his range of vision. He fought off the lethargy of cold and blindness, the urge to stop and fall into the snow, sleep forever.

Jed was dropping farther and farther back, stiffened with a growing chill that sought his bones like a creeping sickness. He, too, suffered with red-rimmed eyes, a hallucinatory blindness that made small objects large, the big ones small. Trees danced on the outer edge of his vision, rose up to the sky and sank like out-of-focus kites at the corners of his eyes. He dozed, woke up, startled, afraid, gripping the saddle horn with desperate fingers. His gloves felt as if they were made of iron. Cold iron. His toes sent shoots of pain up through his legs, to his shins as if he was walking on red-hot spikes. He wriggled them inside his boots and felt a tingling ache that mingled with the other pain until his brain screamed out with the distant pain.

Esquire whickered.

Gunn reined up, listened.

The horse's ears tautened into quivering cones, twitched to pick up sound.

Jed looked up, saw Gunn stopped, hauled back on his own reins. The mules came to a restless halt.

Gunn twisted in the saddle, looked at Randall and shrugged.

The silence stretched into moments. Still, the animals stiffened, listening.

The first indication that something was wrong came a few moments later.

Ahead, from a distance, Gunn heard a shout.

And then, the mountains boomed with explosion.

Reece Parker finished checking all the caps, uncoiled the fuse. He gave himself thirty seconds.

"Y'all get on back with Tolly," he told Brownie and Suggs. "When I light this bastard, you better be under cover."

The men mounted up, rode back behind the sled.

Packer got on his horse, rode to the end of the fuse. He looked back, judged how fast he had to ride to get out of the way. He was hoping the explosion would blow the snow outward, the drifts absorbing most of the concussion. He had buried the sticks deep. On either side were twelve foot drifts.

He struck a match, sucked in a breath.

"Look out!" he yelled, lighting the fuse.

The fuse caught, hissed. He dropped it like a poisonous snake, kicked his spurs into his horse's flanks, turning him. The sparks raced down the fuse, as Packer counted. He passed Tolly huddled behind the sled, passed Suggs and Brownie, leaped out of the saddle, buried himself deep in a snowdrift. Counting.

". . . twenty-three, twenty-four . . ."

He got up to thirty, started to get up. The last

second seemed to last for an eternity.

Then, the explosion rocked the stillness. There was a muffled whump, then a deeper boom as the other sticks exploded. The air was filled with snow, rocks, sticks, antlers, blood, flesh. Stones whistled through the air, deadly as bullets.

The snow on the mountain held.

Tolly looked up into the snowstorm. Flakes sparkled in the weak sunlight. He yelled, "Come on!", scrambled for his seat on the sled. The men chased their horses, mounted up. Miraculously, none were injured, but they were stunned by the noise.

Packer kicked his horse, took the lead. He rode through a fine mist, grinning from ear to ear. He broke the trail for the sled, saw that the dynamite had done its work. The snow drifts were blown to bits, the ground showed through. He gave a hoarse shout and rode fast until deeper snow slowed him down. The way looked clear though. There were no drifts as large as the one they had blasted.

Oro City was close.

Gunn wasted no time. The echoes from the explosion continued for a long time, but he was fighting the drifts, jerking the mule after him. He did not look back, but was sure Randall was doing the same. He figured that Stagg had either blown up the road behind him or cleared a path through impassable drifts. Either way, he had to know.

They rode through an eerie stillness. Flakes of snow still danced in the air. The stench of explosives still hung in the air.

Gunn was relieved. The explosion had caused no avalanche, nor had Stagg blocked the road. When he rode up to the cleared spot, saw the force of the explosion, he knew what had happened.

But there was no time to waste, either. Stagg was ahead of them, and it was sure he must be packing meat, trying to cut them out. Esquire was tired, but they had not far to go. He let him find his own way, urged him over the rough spots.

An hour later, they saw the smoke of the town, the first buildings.

"Alpine House. I'll lead the way."

People came out to stare at them, point at the mules pulling the travois.

"You're a mite late," yelled someone. "Tolly Stagg done beat you in!"

Gunn said nothing, but followed in Randall's wake.

He saw the sled in front of Alpine House. Men on the porch. A woman. They all stared as Randall and Gunn pulled up, halted, their animals blowing steam through straining nostrils.

"Miss Blake," said Randall politely, "we've come with the meat. We got more."

Eloise Blake frowned, looked past Randall at Gunn. Gunn was staring hard at Tolly Stagg who stood next to her on the porch.

"I—I don't know what to say," she said. "I—we didn't think you'd make it through. Mister Stagg here . . ."

"Mister Stagg doesn't have a contract," said Gunn quietly. "This is Lund's meat and I'm delivering it as promised."

Stagg stepped forward.

"You ain't got no business here, stranger."

Gunn shifted his weight in the saddle.

"I reckon I do, since I bought into Lund's outfit," he said.

Reece Packer stepped up beside Tolly. Brownie and Suggs backed into the shadows.

Eloise saw the trouble coming.

"Wait a minute," she said. "I think we can work things out. You all come in, have a drink. We'll talk."

"Fine with me," said Gunn.

"You and me have a deal, lady," said Stagg belligerently. "I come in first. Let this stranger go on to Denver and peddle his meat."

No one would make Denver until the thaw, be it next week or next Spring. Everyone there knew that. Tolly was throwing down a challenge. He had three men to back him up. Gunn and Randall were outnumbered.

"Anybody honor contracts in this town?" asked Randall, cutting through the deadly silence.

"Of course," said Eloise. "But we can work out a solution, I'm sure. These are unusual circumstances. If there is any blame, it's to be put on me. Please, gentlemen, come inside. You all must be frozen. The drinks are on the house."

Brownie and Suggs cheered. The tension eased.

Tolly stood his ground, but Eloise touched his arm, whispered to him.

"Please," she said. "I don't want trouble."

"Me neither," said Stagg, "but we was here first."

"You and Mister Packer go inside. I'll be along."

Reece shot a dirty look at Gunn, followed his boss into the hotel. Gunn and Randall dismounted, tied up their horses, the mules. Other buyers crowded around.

"We want in this, Eloise," one of them said. "We got a stake in that meat."

"Yes. Everyone come inside."

She waited for Gunn and Randall to climb onto the porch.

"I don't believe I've had the pleasure," she said. "You must be Mister Gunn."

She held out a hand. Under her coat, he could see that she had fine lines, was every bit as pretty as Randall had said. He took off his frozen glove, touched her hand, half-bowed.

"It's just Gunn," he said. "Miss Blake. Mighty nice to meet you."

She smiled at his courtly manner.

But her eyes flashed an entirely different welcome. She turned away quickly so that he wouldn't notice the flush that rose to her cheeks.

Gunn did notice, however, and he felt the faint flutter of butterflies in his stomach.

Eloise Blake, at that moment, could have had anything she asked for, bar none.

CHAPTER SEVENTEEN

The men crowded the bar at Alpine House. Slim and another bartender served the drinks, as the talk buzzed through the room. Gunn stood away from the pack, watched Eloise get help in putting tables together. Chairs scraped as men took up seats, holding glasses of whiskey or beer.

"Get you something, Gunn?" asked Randall.

"Whiskey."

Eloise Blake motioned for him to come over.

"Sit down, won't you? I think we can settle this quickly."

Tolly Stagg sat at the head of one of the tables, flanked by Reece Packer and Brownie. Packer was one of the few men in the room who was bareheaded. Gunn noted that and curled his lips in a half-smile. Alf Suggs stood in the background, as if ordered there by Stagg. The others in the room crowded around the table, or brought up chairs so they could listen to the talk. Stagg glared at Gunn, sizing him up. Packer licked his lips, sipped whiskey. Bottles appeared on the table. Boots clumped as the men settled down. Jed sat beside Gunn, handing him a tumblerful of whiskey. Gunn set it in front of him, waited for the talk to begin.

"Now, gentlemen," said Eloise, "if we can be quiet for a minute, I think we can work things out. You, Mister Gunn, say you are acting in partnership with the late Grandy Lund's family.

"I am."

"Can you prove that?" asked Stagg.

"Do I have to? Those are his mules out there."

"What happened to Lund?" asked Packer.

Gunn looked him coldly in the eye.

"I killed him," he said.

There was a collective gasp from the spectators, those at the table. Eloise blinked as if she couldn't believe her ears.

"You murdered Grandy Lund?" she asked.

"I didn't say that, Miss Blake. I killed him. In self defence. His daughters will tell you that's the truth."

"But they ain't here," said Stagg.

Voices rose up and Eloise had to bang an empty mug on the table for silence.

"All right, we can straighten that out later. For the moment, sir, we'll take you at your word. I made a mistake. When the blizzard came on us, we had no meat in town. Mister Stagg here offered to bring some in. It was a question of survival. We had no way of knowing how long the storm would last. Now, it appears we have two sellers. Do you, Mister Gunn, have an objection to our buying Mister Stagg's meat along with your own?"

"He better not," said Brownie.

Some of the men laughed self-consciously. Gunn said nothing. Reece gulped his whiskey, narrowed his eyes.

Gunn waited until the snickers and the talk died down. He knew everyone there was expecting an answer. The right answer. If he said the wrong thing, there could be bloodshed. Yet he had an obligation to the Lund girls, to Lund himself. A contract was a contract. Yet he had not fulfilled the contract to the limit. Still, there was time left, and there was more meat back at the Lund cabin. He had to choose his words carefully, be fair, yet at the same time he had to stand firm for the sake of that contract. He took a taste of his whiskey, cleared his throat.

"We packed in almost two ton of elk, deer and antelope," he said quietly. "We've got another ton or so back at Lund's. The due date is three days hence. I can see your position, Miss Blake, and Mister Stagg's too. Now, we have a contract. That's got to hold. But you made an agreement with Stagg there and that ought to hold too."

Voices rose up again and Gunn held up his hand.

"I'm not finished yet. I have an agreement with the Lund women and am acting here as their agent and partner. Our meat must be bought, all of it. If you buy Stagg's meat, then you'll likely have too much and the rest of the meat we bring in will spoil. I'm willing to pay Stagg and his men as hunters, buy their meat and use it towards our contract."

Tolly's face reddened. He slammed a fist down on the table, rattling the bottles and glasses.

"No, by god!" he roared.

The babble of confused voices mingled with shouts of outrage and protest. Eloise tried vainly to silence the men who all wanted to be heard at once. Tolly Stagg rose from his chair, bellowed at them.

"Shut up!" he yelled. The hubbub died down. "Listen, you fools! We beat Gunn here. We have only his word that's he's working Lund's territory. He says he killed the man I believe him. I believe he killed him so's he'd get it all for hisself. For all I know, he may have murdered those gals too! I ain't takin' his cheap word for nothin'. You buy our meat, as agreed. I ain't working for no hunter's wages!"

"Good for you, Tolly," said Packer. "We'll back your play."

Disorder broke out again, but Tolly backed up. Reece and Brownie got to their feet. Alf Suggs drifted out of the shadows, ready.

The talk faded away.

Eloise blanched.

"No!" she said. "No shooting. Listen to me! I'll buy your meat, Mister Stagg, and that's the end of it! Yours, too, Mister Gunn. I want no killing in my place."

"Let's hear what Gunn has to say," said Tolly. "I'm callin' him out. Right here and now."

Gunn looked hard at Tolly Stagg. Jed sat motionless next him. Four guns faced them. At close range. Bullets would fly. A lot of innocent people might get hurt. Or killed. He and Jed were the outsiders here. If push came to shove, they'd go down.

"I say," said Gunn, "we ought to accept Miss Blake's offer, and get that meat unloaded."

A cheer rose up in the room. Someone slapped Gunn on the back. Tolly Stagg glared, but was lost in a rush of men who crowded back to the bar. The tension subsided.

Eloise Blake shot him a grateful look.

Gunn finished off his drink. Jed gave him an idiotic grin and downed his own whiskey.

"Buy you another," said Randall, still grinning idiotically.

"Hell, you didn't buy that one, did you?"

"No, but I sure want to buy something right now. I thought we were goners."

"It would have been tight, Jed. Mighty tight."

Eloise beckoned to Slim, who thundered over, the floorboards creaking under his weight. She whispered into his ear. Tolly Stagg came up to Gunn, looked down at him.

"I ain't finished this deal yet, Gunn," said Stagg, his eyes flashing hatred.

Gunn held his gaze steady.

"You got what you wanted, didn't you Stagg?"

"Not by a damn sight!" he growled, turning on his heel. Reece Parker looked at Gunn, touched a finger to the brim of his hat. A faint smile flickered on his lips.

Slim brought a money pouch to Eloise and she counted out the stacks of bills to pay for the meat. Stagg and Gunn both signed receipts.

"We'll unload you," said Eloise, "and I'll see to it that the other buyers get their share. I wish you gentlemen would shake hands. I really think it worked out fairly for everyone."

"Miss Blake," said Stagg, "I don't shake hands with a man I don't like."

Gunn ignored the statement.

"I'll bring in the rest of the meat in two days, Miss Blake," said Gunn, "barring bad weather or bushwhackers."

"What's that supposed to mean?" asked Stagg.

Gunn looked over at Packer, reached inside his coat. He pulled out the hat he had found on the ridge.

"You can give this to that man over there. I think he's one of your pards."

Packer saw the hat and his face clouded over. Gunn shoved the hat in Stagg's hand.

"I don't know what you're talkin' about," he muttered.

"Your friend does. He left that hat back there on the trail. See that his head don't get cold and give it to him, won't you?"

Stagg stormed away, tossed the hat to Packer.

"What was that all about?" asked Eloise.

"Oh, we've met before is all," said Gunn. "Real recent. I don't know the names of those other men, but I expect we'll meet again."

Eloise told them who they were.

"But I want you and your friend to have supper with me tonight," she said. "You surely won't ride back to Lund's cabin after such a trip?"

"One of us has to," said Gunn.

"I'll go dammit," said Randall, overhearing. "You need some city time. You want me to bring in the rest of the meat, right?"

"You could pack it all right. Goin' back light, you ought to be there a couple of hours after dark."

"I'll have another whiskey and a quick chaw of some elk meat before I go," said Jed.

Gunn tipped his hat to Eloise.

"I'll get my horse taken care of, help Jed with the grub and loading up. See you at supper, ma'am. You got any vacancies at the hotel?"

"We have several," she smiled. "I'll make all the arrangements.

None of them noticed Alf Suggs standing a few feet away. As Gunn and Randall left, he hurried over to where Tolly, Brownie and Reece were standing at the end of the bar. Men carried in chunks of game meat, took them into the kitchen. There was a general air of festivity in the bar, but Tolly Stagg frowned when he heard what Suggs had to tell him.

"I want you to load up what you can, Jed," said Gunn as Randall was ready to ride. "I'll leave in the morning, meet you somewhere along the way. I don't think Stagg's going to let this go by, but we may have gotten over the worst of it."

"I don't trust him or his bunch."

Gunn looked at the sky. It was still overcast, but the wind had died down. There was plenty of snow left. The poles were lashed to the mules and they were strung out on a leadrope. Jed had miles of hard riding to go, but he wanted to get the meat in on time.

"You handle two mules and if that's not enough, I'll go on and bring in the meat that's left. Leave Stagg to me."

"You watch yourself, Gunn."

"I will."

"I mean with that Blake woman. She's got her eye on you."

"Hell, I'll have supper with her and then get some shuteye. Want to leave before daybreak."

"Maybe," Jed grinned. "Maybe you won't want to come back at all."

Gunn slapped Jed's horse on the rump.

"Get out of here," he said.

"See you, Gunn."

Jed rode down the street, leading the mules. Gunn watched him go. He had no way of knowing that Alf Suggs and Brownie had left a half hour before, heading in the same direction.

Kristina rubbed her horse's forelegs with gloved hands. Droplets of ice crunched as they broke free of the fine hairs. Her breath was smoke on the air. The horse snorted, pawed the snow.

"Leni," she said, "you want to take the lead for a while? My eyes feel like they're on fire."

"Sure, Kristina. It'll be easy. But I don't understand these other tracks all of a sudden."

"Someone came through with a sled."

"Who?"

Kristina shrugged. She had been breaking trail for over ten miles and the brightness had made her half-blind. There was a throbbing at the back of her head. She felt as if someone had driven a hammer into the base of her skull. This was the first time they had stopped to rest since leaving the cabin. The trail had been easy to follow, but the snow was so deep she knew the horses were tiring. Perhaps, she thought, they should have stayed back at the house, but she was worried so about Gunn. Now, after coming this distance, she was even more worried. There was a place where he and Randall had stopped for some time. There were odd furrows in the snow, footprints leading up the slope of the mountain. Very odd, she thought. Something had happened at that place. A short distance later, she saw where the two horses had come down the slope, doubled back to pick up the mules. Then, these other tracks. Other horses, a sled.

She didn't like it, but there was nothing she could do about it. Now, the tracks were a maze in the snow and her eyes hurt so badly they were only a blur of blackness against the stinging whiteness that surrounded them on all sides. She felt swallowed up by it, small against the massive coldness of the mountains.

"You—you break trail for a while, Leni. Don't worry if I drop back some. My horse needs to slow down a bit."

Leni laughed. She was exuberant. She made a snowball, threw it at her sister. Kristina ducked, but it hit her in the chest. No harm done. It exploded into powder.

"Let's go," said Leni. "I'll show you what Dob can do."

"Don't hurry. You'll hurt Dobbins' lungs and your own. Just try to take the easiest way."

"Awww, Kristina . . ."

"Please, Leni. I have a headache."

Leni mounted up, started off at a gallop. Her horse slowed in the deep drifts as Kristina gritted her teeth in frustration and anger. Leni was making a picnic of the ride and it was not that much fun. There was something eerie about following all those tracks, not knowing who had been there, what Gunn had been thinking when he came upon them.

She wished Gunn were with her. She missed him. Wanted him. Her heart tugged every time she thought of him. She thought of his strong arms, his hard loins, the smell of him after they had made love. She thought of his pale blue eyes and the way they reflected everything, taking on colors, turning silver at times, dusky pewter at others.

Her horse, a mare she called Cassie, jogged along, finding her way. The journey seemed slow to Kristina, monotonous now that she didn't have to look where she was going. Every so often, she looked up and saw Leni's back, and then she bowed her head, shrouded her eyes to keep out the blinding whiteness of the snow.

Until one moment, she looked up and Leni was gone.

"Leni?" she called.

Ahead, there was a sharp turn in the road. A jutting slope blocked the way beyond.

Kristina kicked her horse in the flanks, stood up in the stirrups to keep her butt from pounding against the saddle.

Then, she heard a scream.

Leni's scream.

Kristina's blood turned gelid with fear.

She reined up, fumbled under coat for the pistol strapped to her waist. She drew it, cocked it. Her face drained of blood and she felt the cold sink through to the marrow of her bones.

"Leniiiiiiiiiiiiiiil" she shrieked.

"Kristina . . . help! Help me!"

The horse balked. Kristina slammed her heels into his flanks, whipped it with the trailing end of her reins. The horse moved ahead. She kept kicking it, holding the pistol up, ready to cock it.

She rounded the bend, and heard a shot.

A bullet whistled by her head.

She cocked her pistol.

Two men flanked Leni and her horse. One of them was aiming his pistol in Kristina's direction. She saw smoke, orange flame and heard its report a split second later. She didn't duck. Then, one of the men grabbed Leni and hit her in the face with his fist. Leni crumpled. He grabbed her, lifted her from the saddle. He threw her face down across the saddle, slid up on the cantle.

Kristina, her heart in her throat, brought her pistol down, drew aim on the man shooting at her and squeezed the trigger. Her horse jumped, almost unseating her. The explosion echoed in the dry windless air. The bullet kicked up a puff of snow a dozen feet in front of the other man. He returned fire and Kristina felt a tug at her coat.

Something wet dripped from her arm. She swayed dizzily in the saddle, suddenly sick to her stomach.

She squinted through the white brightness, through the dazzling light and tried to see the man dancing a hundred yards away. She cocked and fired, without realizing it, felt the pistol buck in her hand. She kept shooting as the two men retreated, carrying away her sister. When her pistol was empty, she kept shooting it, listening, fascinated, to its empty clicks.

And then there was no longer anyone to shoot at.

Leni was gone, kidnapped.

She was alone.

Kristina fought back the tears, but they came anyway. She reached into her coat for bullets, dropped several in the snow before she reloaded her pistol. She kept kicking the horse, but it wouldn't move. She realized, then, that it had been shot. She reached down, touched the sticky blood that was already freezing up, matting on its shoulder. She climbed down from the saddle, looked at the wound.

The bullet had stung the bone, bruised it. There was a furrow through the flesh. She saw the break in her stirrup strap where bullet had severed the leather. She washed the wound with snow.

She wept hysterically.

The silence swallowed up her sobs and she climbed back up in the saddle. "Come on girl, we can make it," she said.

The horse moved.

Kristina headed down the road toward Oro City, the weight of her defeat heavy on her shoulders. Somehow, she had failed, without any understanding of the rules. Something terrible was going on. She had to find Gunn if only to draw comfort from him, ask what they must do. She knew that her sister's kidnapping was somehow connected to Tolly Stagg and his bunch. She hated him now. She wished him dead. Gunn might be able to help. For now, though, she was alone, far from any comfort.

Leni was gone and she had no idea where or why.

CHAPTER EIGHTEEN

The room was plush, the walls flocked with red velvet, patterned with white roses. The lamps burned golden and the candles threw a warm glow over the yellow tablecloth. The plates and silverware gleamed. A bottle of wine sat on a tray, the twin glasses sparkled, reflected the light.

Gunn had been in such rooms before, but not often and not recently.

"I thought we might have more privacy if we dined here," said Eloise Blake. "May I pour you a drink? I'm having brandy myself."

"Whiskey would be fine."

"I'll take your hat." Her voice was low, husky. She took his breath away as she closed the door, took his hat hung it next to the mirror in the alcove. Her hair was combed to a high sheen. She wore a pink dress that fit tightly. When she walked, he could see the briefest flash of ankles adorned in black silk. Her scent was heady, like wildflowers. "Come in and make yourself comfortable. I'm having our supper brought up."

"Mighty nice of you, ma'am."

"Please. Call me Eloise. Or El."

She waved him to the couch, surprised him by

sitting next to him.

Gunn looked at the decanters on the low table. She poured a fine brandy into a snifter for herself, a generous tumblerful of whiskey for him. The tumbler was cut glass crystal.

"Mighty nice room, ma'am. Eloise."

"Thank you. I lived in San Francisco for a time, decorated it in the style of that fair city."

"Why'd you leave, come to a place like this?"

She laughed held up her glass.

"First, a toast. You handled yourself well today. It could have been ugly."

"It was ugly enough." He clinked his glass against hers. They drank, peering at each other over the tops of their glasses. Her eyes danced with shimmering light. She was very beautiful.

"I had an offer," she said, "from a very handsome gentleman. He sent me the fare to Denver. I loaned him money. He ran out on me. I worked for a time there, a favorite aunt died and left me a small sum and I came here when the silver strike made it attractive."

"Did you love the gentleman?"

"I thought I did. I was infatuated with him."

"Ever hear from him?"

"Oh, yes," she laughed. "He came back, begged me for forgiveness."

"And . . .?"

She laughed harshly, tossed her head. Her breasts pushed against her bodice, appeared ready to pop free if she laughed again.

"I don't like weak men. I saw George for what he was. I staked him and he got into a card game. He was shot for cheating."

"You sure pick 'em."

"I was very young then. Barely eighteen."

"And since then?"

"Since then, I've been looking for a real man, Gunn."

He drank quietly, watched her eyes. They didn't waver. He felt her electric presence, the allure she radiated. A mocking smile played on her lips and he wanted to kiss her, to wipe it away. He wanted to crush those melony breasts to his chest, run his fingers through her hair. But this was her room, her play. The whiskey warmed his throat, his belly. He had rested, felt fine, relaxed, ready for anything.

"You have quite a reputation, Gunn. Is it all true?"

"I wouldn't know."

"Some of it must be true."

He shrugged.

"You don't like to talk about the past, do you?"

"No."

"Let's talk about you. Are you hungry?"

"No. Not for food."

She laughed. Her breasts swelled like ripe cantaloupes.

"You talk my language. There's a bell rope over by the wall. When I pull it they'll bring our supper."

"Are you hungry?" he asked bluntly.

She drew in a breath.

"We can always eat. Anytime we want. Your stay will be short, I gather."

"I reckon. I came here because Randall wanted to see if he could become a millionaire in a silver mine. Overnight."

They laughed together.

"Is that the only reason you came here?"

"It was a place to come. I have no home."

She moved closer to him, set her glass down on the table. He set his glass down, as well, waited for her to make a move. She had set the stage, but he was one of the players. Once she lifted the curtain, he would act out his own role. Eloise was a desirable woman. Hungry. Her eyes showed it. She was no tramp, but she was lonely. He knew the look. He knew what it was to be in her shoes.

"You might want to stay here," she said. "There are opportunities. Oro City will grow. It will become important. Soon, I think. Already, there is talk of building, schools, churches. A regular town."

"I've been in regular towns. They go through the same pains. They grow, they die, they get too fancy, too civilized."

"You don't, though, do you, Gunn?"

Her voice was a husky whisper. She was close, very close.

"Huh?"

"You don't get civilized."

Her fingernails touched the back of his hand, then. She scraped a finger down a vein. His skin tingled with her faint touch. Her lips were wet, inviting. She leaned closer to him. He reached out, curled a hand around the nape of her neck. He drew her toward him. She did not resist.

"No, I don't," he said, gruffly. "Is that what you like? Civilized, gentlemanly behavior?"

"I had that," she husked.

"Don't pull that bell rope," he said, drawing her to

him. He kissed her on the lips she offered him, slow and easy at first. She squirmed against him, mashing her lips against his. She panted with desire. He touched her breast, the soft flesh that was exposed. She winced, writhed. He squeezed her mound, then, crinkling the cloth. She gasped, slithered her tongue inside his mouth.

He felt her hands grasping him, kneading his shirt, twisting, groping, searching him out. She touched her tongue with his, felt her flinch as if electrified.

"Gunn," she breathed. "Take me. Take me to bed."

"Yes."

The two riders were on him before he could move out of the way.

Jed recognized them.

The two men who had been with Stagg. But someone else was with them too, someone across the saddle of one of them.

"Hold up!" Jed yelled.

Alf Suggs drew his pistol, fired.

Jed ducked, dropped the rope. The mules scrambled. He felt one of them smash into his horse as he clawed for his pistol.

Brownie stopped, drew his rifle.

Leni screamed in terror.

"What the hell you doin' with her?" Randall asked. "Leni?"

Suggs came on, fast, firing as he rode. Jed jerked his pistol free, cocked it.

A bullet slammed into one of the mules. It fell against Jed's leg, knocking his horse sideways. He fired, missed. His bullet whined harmlessly into the air. His horse spun around.

Brownie took aim with the rifle, fired. The barrel exploded with smoke, flame. The lead ball smashed into Jed's horse. The horse went down.

"Ride on, Alf!" yelled Brownie. "He's done for!"

Suggs, carrying Leni, rode past the floundering mules, hell bent for leather. The mule that was hit kicked wildly, its blood staining the snow. Jed was pinned under his horse. It was quivering in its death-throes. The impact had knocked him almost senseless. He tried to see, but all he heard was the pound of hooves on snow.

Brownie fired twice more as he rode by. Jed buried himself behind his horse, heard the bullets thunk into the animal. The horse stopped quivering, lay still, its weight crushing Jed's leg. The sky swam and pain shot through his hips when he tried to move.

After awhile, it was quiet.

Jed felt the cold seep into his bones. He touched the part of his leg that was not under the horse. It didn't feel broken, but it was going numb fast. He twisted, to bring his other leg up, to try and kick the horse up enough to pull his leg free. He wrenched his hip, doubled over in excruciating pain. Sweat oozed from the pores on his face, froze almost instantly.

He swore, helpless, frustrated.

He lay there for a long time, wondering how long it would take him to die. His leg no longer hurt. He thought that it would be the part to die first. Soon it would be night and the temperature would drop. That would be the end of him. A mule, tangled in the rope, brayed forlornly.

Jed tried to sit up, fell down, exhausted.

He waited for the cold to kill him.

"I thought I'd have to seduce you," she whispered.

Gunn started unbuttoning the back of her dress. He peeled it off her, looked down at her creamy breasts. She worked at his belt, unbuckling it.

The bedroom was bathed in lamplight. The covers lay turned back, the sheets inviting.

"No. You just had to be willing," he husked.

She stepped out of her dress, finished opening his trousers. They slid to the floor. She undid his shirt bared his chest.

"I was willing the first moment I saw you, Gunn."

They hurried. He took her to bed, lay her on the soft white sheets. He looked at her, drank in her beauty. He rubbed her tummy. She touched his chest, raked it with her fingernails, gently, teasingly. Her eyes swept over his naked body. She touched his rigid cock, pursed her lips.

"You're quite a man. I've been waiting a long time to meet someone like you."

He stroked her breasts, tweaked the nipples between thumb and forefinger. They hardened into rubbery buttes of dark flesh. He leaned down, suckled them, first one, then the other. She squirmed against him, squeezed his manhood, compressing the swollen veins. He felt her fingernails scrape lightly against his scrotum.

He kissed her all over her body and she grew more willing with each new exploration of his mouth and tongue. She twisted around, slid down his leg and took his throbbing organ into her mouth. She drew him

187

deep inside, laved the seep-sogged crown with her tongue. Gunn felt as if he was being turned inside out. He wanted her. He wanted her so bad he could hardly stand the terrible wait.

He buried his head between her legs, burrowed into the dank thatch that shielded her sex. His tongue found her, dipped into the honeypot until she arched her back and sighed, screamed something he couldn't understand. They clawed at each other, sipped at one another's secret places and burned like raw flesh on a spit with desire for each other.

"Gunn—Gunn I can't stand it anymore. I—I want you so much, my darling. My big sweet man!"

He brought her around. She was light as a feather. His musk was still thick in his nostrils and now he looked at her shining face. He straddled her, sank to her quaking loins. She pulled at his cock, guided him to her love-slit. When he penetrated the swollen lips of her cunt, she gasped, shuddered with a jolting orgasm. Her fingernails dug into his arms, the muscles.

"Oh, yes, Gunn, yes," she breathed.

Kristina's breath caught in her throat.

The dark was coming on and she heard a strange sound.

Her horse was limping badly and the last few miles had taken their toll on her strength and patience. The light was fading and only the snowgleam held her to the trail. She knew she was close to Oro City, but now, the landmarks, hard enough to determine after the blizzard, were becoming elusive.

A scratching sound. A wheeze.

She moved ahead, cautiously, steadying her horse.

A low moan reached her ears.

Several yards further on, she saw a dark shape loom on the trail. Instinctively, she reached for her pistol, lifting her coat, touching a gloved hand to the butt.

"Who's there?" she called softly. Her voice squeaked in her throat. Squeaked from fear. "I'll shoot if you don't answer."

There was no answer.

She gently nudged her lame horse with her heels, tapping its flanks with spurless boots. The mountains rose up to the sky, shutting off the weak light from the sun, but she saw the shape move. She recognized it as a mule, one of her father's.

She rode on, heard the poles rattle as the mule trotted toward her.

Her finger touched the trigger guard of her pistol, found the trigger. She started to draw when another sound made her pause.

"Oooohhh," moaned someone.

Kristina rode past the lone mule, avoiding the travois poles that jutted beyond its rump. A pair of mules stood motionless, entangled in rope, next to the slope. The moan had come from another direction.

She saw Randall's horse, then. Her heart caught in her throat. Her stomach boiled with butterflies.

"Jed? Is that you?"

Beyond the still hulk of his horse, she saw another shape. Coming closer, she made it out to be a mule. Dead, from the look of it.

The air was still. It was cold. The soundless presence of mountains towered over her. She felt very small.

"Jed? Gunn?"

There was a noise, like a breath being drawn in. Then, a low groan that seemed to come from somewhere near Jed's horse.

"Help me! Help me!"

"Jed! I'm coming!"

Kristina dismounted quickly, ran to the dead horse. In the dim light she saw Jed Randall lying there, pinned down by the animal's frozen bulk. She ran around to him, knelt down, lifted his head.

"Jed! It's me, Kristina!"

His teeth chattered, and his lips moved, but no words came out.

She assessed the situation quickly. Something terrible had happened. Jed was hurt, near death. His skin felt deathly cold to the touch. His lips were dry, his eyes dull as stone.

"Kristina . . . my leg . . ."

His voice was weak, his complexion gray as ashes. She slapped his face, rubbed his near-frozen hands. She felt his leg, the one that was pinned under his dead horse. He didn't flinch. Her heart sank. There was a danger here. A danger of gangrene, of mortification. He might die. Suddenly, her own troubles seemed very minute, very inconsequential. She knew she had to do something and do it fast.

"Jed, I'm going to try and get your leg free. You've got to help me."

"It's so dark and warm," he babbled.

She slapped his face.

"Pay attention. Help me. The horse is frozen, dead. Your leg is way underneath it. It's very heavy. You have to sit up, push with your other leg. Do you

190

understand me?"

"I'm going back to sleep, lady. I'm too far gone . . ."

His voice was weak. She tried lifting the horse. It was no use. She bit her lip. Jed's head had fallen back onto the snow and his eyes were closed. The light was fading fast. She sat back on her haunches and thought hard. She looked at the milling mules and an idea struck her.

Quickly, she got up, ran to the mules, worked one of the travois poles loose. She dragged it to Jed's horse. She shoved one end under the animal, close to where Jed's leg was pinned.

Summoning her strength, she walked under the pole, lifting with her hands. She shoved and grunted.

"Jed!" she yelled. "You've got to wake up! Move your leg. Pull it out with your hands!"

Randall raised his head, stared at her groggily. She continued to yell at him. Finally, he seemed to realize what she wanted.

"My leg?"

"Yes, when I lift the horse, pull it out quickly. Jed! Do it!"

"Do it," he repeated, dully.

"Now!" She ran under the pole, pushing with all her might. The horse lifted slightly and Jed grabbed his thigh with both hands, pulled his leg free. It began to tingle as the blood rushed back into the veins. He cried out in pain, shreiked with agony as feeling returned to the crushed limb.

Kristina dropped the pole, went over to help Jed restore circulation to his leg. She rubbed it vigorously as he writhed in pain.

"Jed, listen to me! Did you see Leni?"

"Yes. Two men. Took her. Shot at me. Killed my horse."

"We have to find Gunn. Can you stand up? Can you walk?"

He nodded weakly.

"Let me help you. We can ride double. My horse is hurt, but I think we can make it. We must! It'll be dark soon. We have to find Gunn. Do you understand?"

"Kristina, if I can get to walkin' my blood will come back. Nothin's broke. Help me up. Jesus, I thought I was gone."

She hugged him impulsively, helped him struggle to his feet. He lurched and she held onto him. She put an arm over her shoulder.

"We can make it," she said. "It's not far. But we have to hurry."

Her horse held steady as she approached. She knew that Jed was in bad shape, but he was alive. She was alive. They had to get to Oro city and find Gunn. He would know what to do. Leni's life was at stake. The men who had taken her meant to use her for some dire purpose. She shuddered to think about it. But now, for the first time since Leni had been taken, she felt a faint glowing coal of hope.

Jed made it into the saddle.

Kristina swung up in front of him.

"Hold on," she said. "We're going to find Gunn and my sister."

Jed swayed groggily in the saddle.

He felt sick. His leg was still numb. The dark was coming on and he was chilled to the bone. He wanted to believe Kristina. He wanted to believe that they would find Gunn and everything would be all right.

But in his heart, he knew he was bound to die, one way or the other.

CHAPTER NINETEEN

Tolly Stagg paced behind the stone wall, peering over it impatiently as the sky began to turn dark. The sun had dipped over the far mountain ranges a few minutes ago, but there was still a pale glow in the sky. He flapped his arms to drive off the chill. He looked back at his cabin, saw the smoke rising from the stone chimney. It was warm inside, but he had been checking his defences, looking for Reece to get back from Oro City. He didn't expect Brownie and Suggs back tonight. They had a long hard ride to get to Lund's place. Still, the daylong freeze had put a hard crust on the snow. The boys should have had an easier time of it than they had had when the snow was fresh, powdery. If they made it through, without trouble, they should be able to bring at least one of the girls back by late morning.

That little bitch, Leni—that's the one he wanted. She had killed a good friend, shamed him. If it ever got out . . . well, things had gone beyond that now. Leni Lund was the bait for bigger game. Gunn.

Tolly's cabin was set back from a stream, well-fortified with a rock wall in front, steep shale behind. Nearby was a petered-out mine. He had forced the owner and builder of the cabin out. The road leading to it was steep. Below, he could make out the buildings of the town, the chimney smokes rising in the air. The road twisted and turned, but there were stretches where he could see whoever chose to ride his way. It was an ideal fortress.

Packer had been sent to see what room Gunn had taken, keep track of his movements. Gunn was a damned thorn in his side. No one had bought the idea that Gunn had murdered Grandy Lund, but that was still something that might be used to advantage. Packer hated Gunn, too, but for different reasons. Those reasons weren't important. Not now. Gunn stood in the way of a very lucrative deal. Once he was out of the way, the Lund girls would pack up and leave the country. They couldn't run Grandy's business. They were just females and not much account in this matter.

Tolly stopped, listened. Someone was coming. He peered over the wall, expecting to see Reece Packer. Instead, a pair of riders, coming slow. He stepped onto a flat stone behind the wall so that he could see over it.

"Ho Tolly!"

Brownie!

"Come on up, Brownie!"

A few moments later, Brownie and Suggs rode up. Suggs had one arm around Leni Lund. She was now sitting in the saddle, in front of Suggs. He had his hand up inside her coat. The horses blew, clouding the air with steam. One of them spraddled and let droppings fall.

"You got one of 'em. Quick work."

"They was headin' Tolly, both of 'em." Alf shoved Leni out of his saddle. She caught the saddle horn, slid down the horse's side.

"What about the other'n?"

"She's a spitfire, that'un, Tolly. We'uz lucky to've brung this'un in."

"Yair, fine, Brownie. You boys did fine. Well now, Leni, you don't look so goddamned smart-alecky right now, do ye?" Tolly grabbed her arm, jerked her around so that she faced him.

"Leave me alone, Tolly Stagg!"

"Now, you little bitch, you're gonna start makin' up some for what you did to Carp. Shoes on the other foot now, ain't it?"

Leni spit square into Stagg's face.

He hauled off to strike her when they all heard hoofbeats.

"Somebody's comin'," said Suggs.

"See who it is, Alf," said Tolly. Then to Leni, "I ain't finished with you yet."

"Just wait'll my sister Kristina gets here," said Leni defiantly. But she was trembling inside.

Alf looked over the wall, peered hard down the trail. The light was almost gone, but he could see enough.

"It's Packer," he said. "He's by hisself."

"Good. That means we're just about ready."

Packer rode up, saw the girl, grinned.

"Well, you got one of 'em," he said. "What about Randall?"

"He's likely dead," said Brownie. "We run acrost him. Shot his horse dead, one of the mules. We didn't linger none."

Tolly was impatient for Packer's report.

"What'd ya find out, Reece? About that Gunn."

"Oh, he's holed up all right. Got him a room and everythin'. But he's with the Blake woman, up in her digs. Mighty quiet in there."

The men guffawed lewdly. Leni's face scorched, turned crimson. No one noticed. Her heart began to beat faster. Wisely, she decided to keep her mouth shut. These men would do anything to get even with Gunn, she felt, and she didn't want them to use her against him. But now, it dawned on her why she was there.

They were going to use her as bait to lure Gunn out in the open—kill him!

Eloise bucked and thrashed as her body rippled with orgasm. She had lost track of how many times she had climaxed. Gunn's muscular body was sleek with sweat and he seemed tireless. She kneaded the tough sinews in his arms, held on as he plumbed to the deepest part of her, sending shivers of pleasure through her body.

"Gunn—Gunn, you marvelous creature," she sighed. "I've never been made love to so wonderfully."

"It's my pleasure," he said softly.

Her steaming sheath enclosed him like an envelope. She used muscles to squeeze him like few woman could. Heat drenched his loins. She gripped him tightly inside her, moved her hips in rhythmic counterpoint to his thrusts. He had lost all track of time, but this was the second time they had made love with only a cigarette for him in between. She was insatiable and there was no mention of pulling the bell cord.

"Do it, now, Gunn!" she moaned. "Come, come."

He was ready.

She threw her legs up high in the air. Gunn plunged deep, stroked her fast, burying his shaft clear to the mouth of her womb. She grasped him around the shoulders, held on for dear life. He pinned her to the bed, probed her with quick stabs until her mouth opened wide and she screamed. Their bodies slapped together and he felt the hot pleasureable rush of his semen bursting from his sac.

"Now!" he gruffed.

"Yes, oh yes, now Gunn, now!" she shrieked. Her fingernails, like talons, raked his back. She thrashed in a spasmodic release. He shuddered, spewed his seed into her.

He hung there for mindless moments, even as someone pounded frantically on Eloise's door. For an eternity he couldn't separate the sound from the throbbing blood in his temples. Finally, they both realized that someone was knocking at the door.

"Who can that be?" Eloise asked, her voice faint and faraway as if she had been drugged.

"Sounds mighty urgent."

"You'd better get dressed," she said, a tone of anger in her voice. "I'll see what they want, send them away."

She got up, climbed across Gunn, kissed him quickly on the lips. She put on a robe as he watched her.

"Get dressed," she said again, "just in case."

The knocking got louder.

She left in a whisper of cloth as Gunn slid from the bed, searched for his clothes. As he dressed he heard voices. The hackles rose on the back of his neck as he recognized them.

Jed! Kristina!

"Gunn, you'd better come here!" Eloise called.

He strapped on his gunbelt, strode from the room.

Kristina's mouth opened in surprise. She looked half-frozen. Jed sagged in a chair, was massaging his right leg.

"They've got Leni!" wailed Kristina. "Gunn, they took her! Tolly's men."

"Shot at me, left me for dead," added Randall.

Gunn cursed.

"Where?"

"I'll show you," said Eloise. "Let me get dressed."

She left the room. Kristina stared at Gunn, raked him up and down with accusing eyes. He looked at her steadily, felt her pain.

"Sorry," he said, without defining his meaning. "We'll get her back."

"I—I'm scared, Gunn."

He went to her, took her in his arms. He felt her trembling through the coat she wore. She did not weep, but he knew she wanted to, needed to. He glanced over her shoulder at Jed, who looked up at him, shrugged.

"Tell me what happened, Jed."

Randall told him everything he knew. Gunn got his hat off the rack, put it on. Kristina stood there, wringing her hands. When Eloise returned, she was dressed for the cold.

"It's not far, but it's dangerous," she said. "Tolly Stagg has a well-defended cabin above the town. He's probably waiting for you to ride up there, Gunn."

"I have no choice," he said. "Jed, you feel up to it?"

"Yeah. I'm all right. A little stiff in the leg."

"I'm coming too," said Kristina.

"I'll get a rifle," said Eloise. "Gunn, get your coat, meet us downstairs in the lobby. I'll have our horses saddled."

"We'll need four fresh ones," said Jed. "Kristina's horse is lame and mine's dead."

Gunn left them, his face drawn to a grim tightness. It was bad, awful bad. He didn't give Leni much chance. Tolly Stagg held all the cards. He was the dealer.

By the time the odd foursome was saddled up and ready to ride, most of the town knew what had happened. The miners grumbled, argued, swore as they watched Gunn and the others ride out. Their muttering continued as tempers flared. None of them gave much of a damn for Tolly and none held with kidnapping a woman, a young woman like Leni. It was bitter cold, though, and they were not quick to make a decision to help.

Gunn followed Eloise's lead.

"You just point it out when we're close," he said. "Jed and I will figure out how to get up there."

She described the cabin, the wall, to him as they rode.

The climb was steep and there were no lamps showing up the hill. The dark was pitch and if Eloise had not led the way, Gunn knew they would have a hard time finding Tolly's cabin.

Eloise stopped, whispered to Gunn.

"It's just ahead. What are you going to do?"

"I don't know. Maybe Tolly's not here."

Then, he heard someone cough. A boot scraped.

"They're here," said Eloise softly.

Gunn told the women to stay behind. He and Jed, dismounted, slid their rifles carefully out of their scabbards. His boots crunched on snow. There was no way to get up there without making noise. He motioned for Jed to flank right, indicating he would take the left.

Kristina sat her horse, her rifle across the bow of her saddle. Eloise did the same, as the two men made their way toward the cabin.

Gunn and Randall had gone no more than ten paces apiece when the first shot broke the stillness. The boom of a big bore rifle made the horses jump. Orange flame lit up the night.

"Take cover!" yelled Gunn, hurling himself headlong, cocking his Winchester as he fell.

The other guns on the wall spoke, spewing deadly lead. Bullets ripped through the snowcrust, peppered Gunn's face with wet pulverized snow. He fired at one of the orange bursts of flame, rolled. Men shouted. Leni screamed, then was silenced as if struck with a blow.

Jed got up, ran a zig-zag pattern toward the wall.

Gunn saw his shadowy form and began firing as fast as he could lever and squeeze. He got up on his feet, ran hunched over. His rifle emptied and he dropped it, jerked his Colt free of its holster.

A man stood up to fire down at him, his silhouette just above the wall. Gunn fired, dropping him. The man screamed, tumbled headlong.

"Get Gunn!" yelled Tolly.

Kristina and Eloise started shooting.

"Be careful!" said Eloise, "we might hit Gunn and Jed!"

Jed made it to the wall, counted to five and then dove over. Bullets flew everywhere. Gunn stepped on Alf Suggs' body, the man he had shot off the wall.

Then he dove headfirst over the wall, hit the snow headfirst, rolled in a somersault. He came up shooting. A flash of powder lit Reece Parker's face for a split second. Gunn held on him, belly high, squeezed. His pistol bucked in his hand. Reece screamed, flailed the air as the lead ball slammed into his gut.

Jed Randall went down on his injured leg.

Morton Brown appeared out of nowhere, a shotgun in his hands. He fired pointblank at Randall. Both barrels exploded. Buckshot ripped into Jed's flesh, drove him into the snow, bleeding mortally from a dozen wounds.

Gunn saw it happen.

He cried out in rage, fanned his pistol.

Brownie danced like a rag doll being shredded to bits as the slugs hammered into his body, gouging out chunks of flesh. He pitched headlong, the shotgun flying from his hands.

Kristina, unable to stand it any longer, kicked her horse.

"Come on!" she yelled. "We've got to help Gunn!"

Eloise needed no urging. She galloped after Kristina. They flew off their horses at the wall, climbed over. In the distance, the angry murmur of a mob drifted up the mountain.

Gunn whirled, opened the gate of his Colt, began

ejecting empty hulls. He crouched low, shoved in fresh bullets. His eyes searched for Tolly Stagg.

A shape rose up and Gunn cocked his pistol.

"Gunn — Gunn, look out!"

It was Leni!

From his left, Tolly Stagg fired a rifle from the hip. The explosion lit up Kristina and Eloise, Leni's fear-frozen face. Gunn dropped to his belly, took aim with the Colt. Even as he fired, he knew he was shooting too low.

Tolly twitched as the bullet caught him in the leg. But he did not go down. Instead, he raced toward Leni.

"No!" she screamed.

Gunn tried to swing on Stagg, but he was off-balance. Kristina, however, brought her rifle up, took aim, led Stagg and fired. He staggered as the bullet caught him under the armpit.

He twisted around, aimed at Kristina.

Gunn stood in a single smooth motion, fired his pistol with both hands. Steadied, squeezed.

Tolly went down.

Twitched in agony as Gunn stood over him with smoking pistol.

"Was it worth it, Stagg?"

"Fuck you, Gunn."

"Some bastards die hard," said Gunn, shoving the barrel of his pistol in Stagg's face. He squeezed the trigger. The front of Tolly's face disappeared in a cloud of blood and mangled bone.

The night sky danced with the light of torches.

The miners, armed to the teeth, came up the road like a winding serpent, a mass of men finally able to act. They gathered around the scene of carnage, viewed the dead bodies with masked faces flickering in the blazing light of the torches.

Gunn lifted Leni to her feet, wiped her face. Kristina took her sister in her arms. Then Gunn went to Randall, knelt down beside the body of his friend.

"Ride easy, son," he said quietly, choking back the tears.

He stood up, turned at the sound of sobbing.

"Gunn. Come here. It—it's Leni. She—she's . . ."

Leni sagged in Kristina's arms. Blood oozed from her mouth. Gunn took her in his arms, felt her coat, underneath.

"Stagg—shot me," she said slowly. "He—just shot me for no reason."

Gunn's hands came away, sticky with blood. Kristina began sobbing louder than before. She looked at Gunn's face, lit by torchlight. He shook his head. Leni died in his arms.

"I'm sorry, Kristina," he said, his pale blue eyes brimming with tears. "She's gone. First Jed, now Leni."

The miners heard, saw. Their voices murmured, rose in pitch. Then, they went berserk. They swarmed over the dead bodies of Stagg and his men. They set fire to his cabin. The screamed and yelled their vengeance. They tore Stagg's body to pieces, knifed it into wolfmeat.

Gunn lifted the body of Leni in his arms.

Kristina put her hand on his arm. Together, they walked down the mountain, past the torches of those still coming, bent on vengeance.

Eloise stared after them for a long time. She sighed

heavily and her lips trembled as she voiced his name.

Gunn did not hear her.

He heard only the hollow silence of his own grief, the crunch of his boots on the snow.

Soon, the blood cries of the enraged miners dwindled and faded as the frosted hills swallowed the last echoes of their shouts.

The ashes of victory were bitter in Gunn's mouth. Jed was gone. He would never ride with Gunn again.

For Gunn, the final sadness was the loss of a good friend.

THE END